Tweet Heart

{a novel in e-mails, blogs, and tweets}

Elizabeth Rudnick

HYPERION

NEW YORK

Printed in the United States of America
First Edition
10 9 8 7 6 5 4 3 2 1

Designed by Elizabeth H. Clark
This book is set in 10.5-point Helvetica Neue Light.

ISBN 978-1-4231-3528-9
V475-2873-0-10105
Visit www.hyperionteens.com

To Mom, for everything

Lots0love is now following **ClaireRBear**

Thursday, March 11, 9:02am

 Lots0love@ClaireRBear Welcome to Twitter, Bear! Let the boy-stalking (ahem, following!) begin.

9:02am

ClaireRBear is now following **WiseOneWP**

9:10am

ClaireRBear is now following **KingofSlack**

9:11am

 ClaireRBear@Lots0love HI!!! Me? Stalking boys? Never!

10:07am

 Lots0love@ClaireRBear I can think of one possible exception. His name has the letters J and D.

11:31am

 ClaireRBear@Lots0love Lots, you know me too well. Seriously, don't think I'll survive two weeks without you.

11:34am

KingofSlack is now following **ClaireRBear**

11:35am

 ClaireRBear@Lots0love I bet Italy's beautiful. Why are you tweeting and not out exploring?

11:35am

 Lots0love@ClaireRBear just taking a little "siesta" as they say here in Venice . . . so many gorgeous guys here I've already forgotten about whatshisname.

11:40am

ClaireRBear@Lots0love I think siesta is Spanish, chica. And do you mean Dave? I thought we liked Dave?
11:40am

 Lots0love@ClaireRBear Alas, it was not meant to be. He was a nose breather.
11:45am

 ClaireRBear@Lots0love Isn't everyone?
11:45am

 Lots0love@ClaireRBear Not like Dave they're not. The dude sniffed oxygen like it was going out of style.
11:50am

 Lots0love@ClaireRBear So my search continues. And you know I love the search.
11:51am

 ClaireRBear@Lots0love And I enjoy watching from the sidelines.
11:53am

 Lots0love@ClaireRBear Claire Rachel Collins! You would enjoy said search yourself if you ever tried it!
11:59am

 ClaireRBear@Lots0love I'm just very selective. :)
11:59am

 Lots0love@ClaireRBear I know, little bear. It's what makes you so lovable.
12:01pm

ClaireRBear@Lots0love Oh yeah, that's me. Miss Lovable . . .
12:02pm

 Lots0love@ClaireRBear You know you're adorbs. I'd love to stay and chat . . . but I'm off to meet some Italians. Ciao!
12:14pm

 ClaireRBear@Lots0love K, bye. Talk later?
12:15pm

WiseOneWP is now following **ClaireRBear**
1:23pm

 ClaireRBear@Lots0love Lots? You there?
4:14pm

 ClaireRBear@Lots0love Hello?
4:25pm

 ClaireRBear@Lots0love Sigh. Fine then. Abandon me and frolic with Italians. JK. You know I love ya. Have fun!
4:30pm

3

From: **ClaireBearR16@gmail.com**
Sent: Saturday, March 13, 2:33pm
To: LottieM17@gmail.com
Subject: Come home!

Alright, Charlotte May. If I don't hear from you soon, I'm going all CSI on you and putting out an APB. I need my best friend back—live and in person.

Since you left for your uber-fancy trip (um, can I steal your parents?), I've been at the barn with Maverick or at Bennett's. That's it. I mean, don't get me wrong, I love my horse and Bennett is my boy—but chilling with a guy you used to steal toys from in the paddle pool isn't exactly a thrill. Will P. has been around too, so that's at least helped mix things up a bit. Though most of our conversations revolve around the relative merits of Star Wars vs. Star Trek. I swear, L, if I have to hear another argument over whether Captain Kirk could take Luke, I might go mad. Or start speaking Klingon. It's a fine line. You see why I need you back?

One mini disaster to report: I cut my hair. And got highlights. I blame YOU for the mop on my head. If you had been here you would have told me this was not a good idea. All I wanted was auburn highlights—like in that picture of Scarlett J. you showed me—and just a few layers. I now have fire-engine red streaks and I'm pretty sure a bowl cut. Seriously Lottie, it's worse than that time you cut my bangs while we waited in line for school pics and told me that uneven was the new even. I still don't think my mother has forgiven you for that.

Speaking of disasters, you will NEVER believe what happened. You know how Pookie Williams has been writing that Dear Know-It-All column for the paper since she was a freshman? Well, apparently, as Miss Hot Shot was accepted to Columbia and can coast, she RESIGNED. Can you believe that? I guess you might, but that's not the crazy thing that happened. Mr. Schaberg asked ME to take over the column. So yeah, from here on out, yours truly will be giving the kids of Watkins Prep advice on love and life on a weekly basis. Do you not see the sweet irony in that? I mean, I've barely had a boyfriend and unless life is what happens in a barn, I'm pretty sure I don't have much of one. You can bet your new Italian leather boots I'm going to be coming to you for pearls of wisdom. I'm kind of freaked out about it. Bennett thought it was hilarious, of course. I actually would prefer he speak in Elvish sometimes.

All this alone time has got me thinking, we only have one more semester left of junior year. Isn't that wild? Then we'll be seniors and then we'll leave South Carolina, go to college, and then . . . what? You'll join a sorority and have an insanely hot boyfriend and I'll probably end up living in the library, alone. Guess not much different from now. But the point is, time is flying by. We need to make the most of this semester. Maybe I'll finally let you try to set me up with the king of seniors, Mr. "I've got Zac Efron hair" Jack Dyson Whitcomb. I mean, what's the worst that could happen? He'll ignore me like he has for the past decade?

See what happens when you go away? I go stir-crazy. I ramble in emails and contemplate foolish pursuits. You NEED to get back here ASAP to distract me with tales of Italian boys, pasta, fine art, and vineyards. Only two more days and counting. Can't wait. Call me as soon as you land. Or tweet or whatever.

xoxo
Lonely in SC

Lots0love Buon giorno, world! I'm back stateside and ready to live la vida loca.

Monday, March 15, 7:30am

 Lots0love Okay, I know those are mixed languages but you get my point. Party!

7:31am

 KingofSlack Did anyone see the trailer for the new Jackson movie? Knocked my socks off

7:36am

 WiseOneWP I hope it knocked off those gross gray ones. You need to get new sox, dude. *RT@KingofSlack Did anyone see the trailer for the new Jackson movie? Knocked my socks off*

7:36am

 Lots0love@ClaireRBear My darling Bear, check out Fabrizio. Emailed you his pic

7:37am

 ClaireRBear Monday mornings after vacation are without question the worst.

7:37am

 ClaireRBear Haircut still looks like something out of a slasher film and my mother chose last night to do laundry. Oh jeans why do you take so long to dry!

7:45am

 KingofSlack Don't forget you have to get your first advice column in, too! *RT@ClaireRBear Monday mornings after vacation are without question the worst.*

7:50am

ClaireRBear Thanks for the boost KingofSlack. I'll get you back. *RT@KingofSlack. Don't forget you have to get your first advice column in, too!*
7:50am

 Lots0love@ClaireRBear How can you be sad when you will see me in a mere hour? Be positive, little miss sunshine!
7:51am

 ClaireRBear@Lots0love I AM :) to see you! Just don't want anyone else to see me!!
7:51am

 Lots0love@ClaireRBear Is it worse than the time I got poison ivy on my face and looked like something even Freddy Krueger wouldn't touch?
7:52am

 ClaireRBear@Lots0love LOL! Maybe not that bad. Thxs L! See you at school in a few!
7:53am

 ClaireRBear@Lots0love PS—Fabrizio? Really? Does he effectively eliminate odors?
8:04am

 Lots0love@ClaireRBear U can't make this stuff up! Sit and Sip after my lacrosse practice? I'll fill you in.
8:05am

 ClaireRBear@Lots0love Most def. I can live vicariously through you. See ya soon!!
8:05am

BIG MOUTH B

Who I am: A guy with a big mouth and lots to say.

Where I am: Attending a prep school down South. Not sure what I'm prepping for, exactly.

What I do: Blog on the interwebz. A lot. Don't leave home without me . . . please?

Welcome back to the Hellmouth, kiddies! Time to rise and shine.

Monday, March 15, 8:15am

Hello my fellow Prepsters! I woke up this morning on our glorious first day back at WP with an unusual feeling in my gut—and no, it was not because of the atomic fire wings that a certain friend of mine whose name starts with W and rhymes with Bill dared me to eat. No, I woke up with this strange feeling because after so many years walking the oh-so-lovely (and clean—good job Mr. Janitor Man) halls of Watkins Prep, I am starting to think about leaving. For newer more exciting waters, you ask? Well, that will be up to the admissions gods, and I have a feeling they may not look favorably upon my wit and those freshman year grades. I honestly thought that using John Connor's struggle against the Terminator as an allegory for the war between the Colonies and Britain was original and thought-provoking.

9

Apparently Mr. Harson is NOT a sci-fi fan. And apparently he also has no sense of humor.

But I digress. As we embark on these last few weeks of school before summer and the bliss that it will bring, I want to continue passing on knowledge that I have picked up during my tenure here in these hallowed halls of learning. For now, I will start you off with just a few nuggets of brilliance . . . but stay tuned for more:

1) When you attempt to ask out your longtime crush who happens to be way hotter than you, do NOT under ANY circumstances look anywhere but in her face. Staring at her boobs does not a date make. Trust me. Also, I'd recommend not sneezing on her either. If you have allergies, man, take medicine.

2) If you make it to junior year (after suffering utter and total humiliation at the hands of said hottie), DO NOT think that a sudden growth spurt means you can ask her out again. You are still a dork. Now you just have gangly limbs and an annoying habit of hitting your head on low-hanging objects and a propensity to sometimes grow what looks like dark mold on your upper lip. Remember: you are still NOT cool. Deal with it.

All right, my loyal followers. That's all I can give you for now. Go forth and be wise—or at least wiser than me.

KingofSlack is now following **Lots0love**

12:01pm

 ClaireRBear Wishing words came as easily to me as they do to Big Mouth.

12:02pm

 ClaireRBear Did EVERYONE go somewhere warm this vacay? I'm only one with skin appropriately spring pale.

12:03pm

WiseOneWP is now following **Lots0love**

12:04pm

 WiseOneWP Pasty is the new tan. *RT@ClaireRBear Did EVERYONE go somewhere warm this vacay?*

12:05pm

 ClaireRBear I'm thinking tan in a can is in my future.

12:10pm

 Lots0love@ClaireRBear Pale looks perfect on you sweet girl. Makes those eyes of yours POP.

12:12pm

 ClaireRBear@Lots0love Thanks, O sun-kissed one. Guess I feel better?

12:12pm

 ClaireRBear@Lots0love I can't believe I forgot to tell you what happened over vacay. It involves you know who! And humiliation.

12:13pm

11

Lots0love@ClaireRBear I'm taking this convo direct. This way not everyone can see what you say. Neat, huh? So what happened with JD??
12:14pm

 ClaireRBear@Lots0love It was horrible. You know how his sister rides at the barn. Her horse is Cosmo?
12:15pm

 Lots0love@ClaireRBear Sure. I mean, didn't know the horse's name but anyhoo. So?
12:17pm

 ClaireRBear@Lots0love SO, JD came to pick her up while I was there. And we were talking. Well, he was talking
12:17pm

 ClaireRBear@Lots0love I was sort of stuttering. But point was we were conversing. And he actually laughed at something I said.
12:17pm

 ClaireRBear@Lots0love And then Jessica Mayers walked down the aisle and did this sort of "Heeey JD, aren't you going to come back to the car? I'm so lonely!"
12:18pm

 Lots0love@ClaireRBear UGH! I hate that girl. She is such a royal you know what! Thank god she is a cheerleader and not on lax team.
12:19pm

 ClaireRBear@Lots0love Back to me please? Anyway, so JD said bye and went to find his sister and then Jessica and I were alone.
12:19pm

Lots0love@ClaireRBear Nothing good can come of that.

12:20pm

 ClaireRBear@Lots0love Right you are. As soon as he was gone she got this look on her face. Like a smirk. And was like . . .

12:21pm

 ClaireRBear@Lots0love That's so sweet! I just love it when JD acts all nice to girls like you.

12:21pm

 ClaireRBear@Lots0love I kinda stared at her AND THEN she said, I just hope you don't read too much into it. Wouldn't want you to get your little ole heart broken!

12:23pm

 ClaireRBear@Lots0love I mean, I know I'm not his type but did she have to be that condescending? You should have heard her say "little ole." Ugh.

12:23pm

 Lots0love@ClaireRBear I think you mean, did she have to be such a beyotch? And the answer is NO!

12:24pm

 Lots0love@ClaireRBear U know what I think? I think she's jealous. Cuz I think JD WOULD like someone like you—you know, with a brain AND cute.

12:24pm

 ClaireRBear@Lots0love You are sweet but she is probably right.

12:26pm

KingofSlack Just got back from cafeteria. Why would they serve okra on the first day back? It's salt in our post-vacay wounds. Mushy green flavorless salt.
12:28pm

 KingofSlack Good thing I didn't want to eat anyway. Just further lost my appetite when I saw the lax guys having burping contest.
12:28pm

 KingofSlack Advise: Going out to lunch is the best option.
12:29pm

 Lots0love@ClaireBear STOP THAT! You are a priceless diamond and Jessica is cubic zirconium. I've gotta grab food. Let's talk later.
12:29pm

 Lots0love@ClaireRBear And chin up Bear. Focus on positive. He talked to you. xoxo
12:30 pm

 ClaireRBear@Lots0love I guess. For the first and last time . . .
12:31pm

14

KingofSlack Love that we can use our laptops in study hall. Foolish foolish administration—u don't know the power u give us!

1:45pm

 WiseOneWP Does anyone actually study in study hall?

1:45pm

 KingofSlack Why would anyone study when they can "work" on computer?

1:46pm

 WiseOneWP Because some people want to get into college. *RT@KingofSlack Why would anyone study when they can "work" on computer?*

1:48pm

 KingofSlack College is a year away. Chill out.

1:50pm

 WiseOneWP You are an idiot. *RT@KingofSlack College is a year away. Chill out.*

1:53pm

 KingofSlack For someone who had to be taught the art of the retweet, my friend is awfully snarky.

1:53pm

 KingofSlack@WiseOneWP Hey buddy, did you check out my most recent post?

1:53pm

WiseOneWP@KingofSlack I missed it. Was being picked on because I'm not a Twitter-savant.
1:53pm

 KingofSlack@WiseOneWP Stop whining. It was genius, man. Too bad I had to suffer through another humiliation for inspiration.
1:55pm

 WiseOneWP@KingofSlack You tried to talk to Jessica Mayers again, didn't you?
1:56pm

 KingofSlack@WiseOneWP Don't those girls know that beneath this goofy exterior is someone honest and generally awesome in every way? I'm a winner dammit.
1:56pm

 WiseOneWP@KingofSlack You? Goofy exterior? NO! Seriously, buddy, their loss.
1:57pm

 KingofSlack@WiseOneWP One day I will rule the world with my wit and then they will come running, just u wait and see.
1:59pm

 WiseOneWP@KingofSlack I know you will Han. And I'll be by your side, your loyal Chewbacca.
2:00pm

 KingofSlack@WiseOneWP You are about as hairy . . . and clueless
2:00pm

WiseOneWP@KingofSlack At least I won't worry 'bout premature balding. You want a scrip for Rogaine?
2:01pm

 KingofSlack@WiseOneWP Hardy har har. Speaking of clueless, u following CC yet? U know I love egging on unrequited love . . .
2:03pm

 KingofSlack@WiseOneWP It's perfect. U can sigh and dream and pine over her every tweet and STILL never get up the nerve to ask her out. That's how it's going to be, right?
2:03pm

 WiseOneWP@KingofSlack There is no unrequited love. I think Claire is cool. That's it.
2:03pm

 KingofSlack@WiseOneWP Dude. In Webster's under unrequited there's a pic of u. Deal w/it.
2:04pm

 KingofSlack@WiseOneWP U should have seen your face during welcome back convocation when she was talking to Lottie about JD
2:04pm

 KingofSlack@WiseOneWP So sad, young Will. So sad. U do realize u have no chance while she's into JD?
2:04pm

 WiseOneWP@KingofSlack He's not that great. Plus, Claire is too smart to seriously fall for such a d-bag.
2:05pm

KingofSlack Sure she is buddy. Sure . . . I'm out. History for dummies is calling and then I gots to write the news.
2:10pm

 ClaireRBear@KingofSlack@WiseOneWP See you guys at the comp lab later! You are my guinea pigs for column. Prepare!
2:10pm

 KingofSlack We can't wait. I know the perfect guinea pig. *RT@ClaireRBear See you guys at the comp lab later!*
2:10pm

 ClaireRBear@KingofSlack Oh really? Do tell. Someone more clueless than me?
2:15pm

 KingofSlack@ClaireRBear Forget about it. I was messing with you. Who could be more clueless about love than you?
2:17pm

 ClaireRBear Shooting my so-called friend a very real glare.
2:19pm

 Lots0love Too much pasta and not enough running this vacay. Tmrw's lacrosse practice is going to be the end of me.
2:21pm

KingofSlack We'd miss you. Really. Loads and loads. *RT@Lots0love Tmrw's lacrosse practice is going to be the end of me.*
2:21pm

 Lots0love@KingofSlack Oh shut it Bennett.
2:21pm

 Lots0love Has serious concerns about her bestie's choice of guy friends.
2:21pm

ClaireRBear Back in the computer lab. No rest for the weary school paper editors.
3:50pm

 KingofSlack Watkins Weekly—what would u do without us to fill your pages?
3:51pm

 WiseOneWP At least we are all in this together.
3:51pm

 ClaireRBear@WiseOneWP Quoting High School Musical again my friend?
3:52pm

 WiseOneWP@ClaireRBear Don't make me pull a Troy and start singing about the basketball article I'm editing at the moment. It wouldn't be pretty.
3:53pm

 ClaireRBear@WiseOneWP As long as you don't dance, feel free to sing away.
3:53pm

 ClaireRBear I apologize now fellow students for the terrible advice you are about to receive
3:55pm

 KingofSlack@ClaireRBear Stop w/pity party. u r going to be fine. As long as no one reads the paper this week.
3:59pm

 Lots0love Knows that her girl is going to rock her new gig. Good luck Bear!
3:59pm

ClaireRBear@KingofSlack NOT helping my dear boy.
4:01pm

 KingofSlack@ClaireRBear I kid. u r going to help the entire school hook up. u r practically a love guru.
4:01pm

 ClaireRBear@KingofSlack Oh just leave me alone. Shouldn't you be on Mugglenet or something?
4:01pm

 KingofSlack@ClaireRBear Somebody's a little touchy aren't they?
4:02pm

 ClaireRBear In my next life, I'm going to make sure my best guy friend does not have a sarcastic sense of humor.
4:03pm

 ClaireRBear@Lots0love Okay Miss. I'm cashing in the friend chips. I need help on column. Need to seem love savvy.
4:30pm

 Lots0love@ClaireRBear You could discuss how long distance is NOT a good idea.
4:35pm

 ClaireRBear@Lots0love You and Signor Fabrizio losing something in translation?
4:36pm

Lots0love@ClaireRBear You could say that. When we are skyping, I can never tell if he's telling me I'm beautiful or saying he thinks I'm a big girl.
4:36pm

 Lots0love@ClaireRBear Still, an accent goes a long way.
4:37pm

 ClaireRBear@Lots0love Cuteness can do the same thing.
4:37pm

 Lots0love@ClaireRBear Ha! Let me guess, you wouldn't happen to mean JD, would you?
4:48pm

 ClaireRBear@Lots0love Why Miss Lottie, why would you ever think that? :)
4:49pm

 Lots0love@ClaireRBear You say the word and I'm on that like white on rice. I can totally hook you two up!
4:49pm

 ClaireRBear@Lots0love OMG! NO! He would never go for me. He's too pretty.
4:50pm

 ClaireRBear@Lots0love It's better if I just leave as is. This way I can pretend he is secretly pining for me.
4:50pm

 Lots0love@ClaireRBear Like you have been pining for him since kindergarten? Or was it pre-K?
4:52pm

ClaireRBear@Lots0love I think it was actually since we were one. I just saw him in that diaper and I knew.
4:53pm

Lots0love@ClaireRBear You are incorrigible. He didn't even move here till we were in pre-K
4:55pm

ClaireRBear@Lots0love That's why you love me so much. :)
4:56pm

KingofSlack@ClaireRBear Keep it down will ya? You type with lead fingers.
4:56pm

ClaireRBear@KingofSlack Yeah? You smell like a gym locker. Leave me alone to think.
4:57pm

KingofSlack@ClaireRBear@Lots0love Lottie—your friend is cranky with a capital C. Come by comp lab and cheer her up please
4:57pm

Lots0love@KingofSlack@ClaireRBear Don't know what you are talking about. She is lovely w/me.
4:58pm

Lots0love@KingofSlack@ClaireRBear And, unlike you bums, I play sports . . . time to go run off ten days of pasta.
4:58pm

ClaireRBear@KingofSlack You are of no use to me right now.
5:00pm

 ClaireRBear@WiseOneWP Hey—you wanna do me a HUGE favor?
5:00pm

 WiseOneWP@ClaireRBear Well hello there. So nice of you to tweet me.
5:01pm

 WiseOneWP@ClaireRBear You do realize I'm sitting right behind you. You could turn around and ask . . .
5:06pm

 ClaireRBear@WiseOneWP Yeah but then I would have to include Benn and point is . . . I don't want to.
5:07pm

 WiseOneWP@ClaireRBear I'm intrigued. Is this something secretive and clandestine? Where did you stash the body? Is it with the money?
5:08pm

 WiseOneWP@ClaireRBear It's OK to tell me. My lips are sealed.
5:09pm

 ClaireRBear@WiseOneWP You are hilarious. But no, this is far more serious than routine murder.
5:10pm

WiseOneWP@ClaireRBear Well in that case . . . Whatever you need.
5:11pm

 ClaireRBear@WiseOneWP YOU GOTTA GET BENNETT OUT OF HERE SO I CAN THINK!
5:13pm

 WiseOneWP@ClaireRBear That I can do.
5:14pm

 ClaireRBear@WiseOneWP Thanks. I owe ya one!
5:18pm

 ClaireRBear First column finally down. How many more to go before Mr. Schaberg pulls the plug?
6:28pm

 ClaireRBear If you want to keep sending questions between issues, check out http://tiny.cc/GyGa5
6:30pm

 ClaireRBear@WiseOneWP Hey, you around?
Monday, March 15, 8:57pm

 ClaireRBear@WiseOneWP Thanks for throwing me a bone with the question, Confused Dude at the Curb. That was you, wasn't it?
8:57pm

ClaireRBear@WiseOneWP Now I guess I just have to wait and see how the column goes over . . .
8:58pm

 Lots0love Heard through grapevine someone isn't as clueless anymore. Congrats on first one done Bear.
9:01pm

 WiseOneWP@ClaireRBear I'm sure you will be a hit! The answers you read me were really funny!
9:06pm

 ClaireRBear@WiseOneWP You HAVE to say that, you're my friend.
9:06pm

 WiseOneWP@ClaireRBear No I don't. Anyway, I'm like Honest Abe—I cannot tell a lie.
9:07pm

 ClaireRBear@WiseOneWP I think that was George Washington, my friend.
9:07pm

 WiseOneWP@ClaireRBear Right. Him, then. I'm honest George. You know history isn't my thing.
9:09pm

 ClaireRBear@WiseOneWP :) Well then, thanks George. Please pass that philosophy on to other boys.
9:10pm

 KingofSlack Does ANYONE care that they pulled Joss Whedon's newest show from TV?? Are they trying to torture me?
9:12pm

WiseOneWP@ClaireRBear Anyone in particular you want me to talk to? Show 'em the ropes?
9:14pm

 ClaireRBear@WiseOneWP Thx Matchmaker, but I got it covered. Don't think JD Whitcomb will listen to ya. No offense.
9:15pm

 WiseOneWP@ClaireRBear Of course. How could I take offense at that?
9:15pm

 ClaireRBear@WiseOneWP You know what I mean. Just JD is JD. Gods don't listen to mortals.
9:16pm

 ClaireRBear@WiseOneWP Really, he's way out of my league. At least according to Jessica Mayers.
9:18pm

 WiseOneWP@ClaireRBear What are you talking about?
9:19pm

 ClaireRBear@WiseOneWP Oh nothing. Just something she said the other day. About JD being too cool for me.
9:20pm

 WiseOneWP@ClaireRBear She's an idiot. He'd be lucky to have someone like you.
9:20pm

 ClaireRBear@WiseOneWP Aw shucks Mr. Parker. Such a flirt! You need a girlfriend!
9:20pm

WiseOneWP@ClaireRBear I do have my eye on someone.
9:21pm

ClaireRBear@WiseOneWP The curiosity is too much. Please tell! Actually, hold that thought. Mom just yelled. I'm supposed to be bonding with her.
9:21pm

ClaireRBear Night, twitterverse. May you all sleep tight.
9:22pm

KingofSlack Seriously people. No more Whedon. Where is the outrage?
9:22pm

WiseOneWP Canceling a TV show? Torture? . . . I can think of worse things.
9:22pm

KingofSlack@WiseOneWP Lemme guess. Fair Claire mess with your heart again?
9:22pm

WiseOneWP@KingofSlack Not intentionally. She is just so hung up on JD. Just brought him up AGAIN.
9:23pm

KingofSlack@WiseOneWP NO! You don't say!
9:24pm

ClaireRBear Oh wait! Posted cute pic of my horse. Had to do it. http://tiny.cc/GyGa5
9:25pm

ClaireRBear Now, for real this time, off I go.
9:25pm

Lots0love I'm going to bed before ten for the first time since I WAS ten. Run wiped me out.
9:29pm

KingofSlack Loser. *RT@Lots0love I'm going to bed before ten for the first time since I WAS ten.*
9:29pm

Lots0love@KingofSlack OMG. Why do you insist on speaking to me?
9:34pm

KingofSlack@Lots0love You know u love it.
9:34pm

 WiseOneWP@KingofSlack Stop picking on Lottie.
9:35pm

 KingofSlack@WiseOneWP Dude, don't get snappy because you're too wussy to tell Claire you like her.
9:35pm

 KingofSlack@WiseOneWP She has been JD this, JD that, JD JD JD . . . since forever. Did u think that would change ever?
9:36pm

 WiseOneWP@KingofSlack I guess I hoped maybe. I mean what would she see in him?
9:39pm

 KingofSlack@WiseOneWP Um, dude—the guy is hot. And capt. of lacrosse team.
9:39pm

 WiseOneWP@KingofSlack That isn't Claire's type
9:41pm

 KingofSlack@WiseOneWP Wasn't done. Capt of soccer team, homecoming king, sings in band . . .
9:41pm

KingofSlack@WiseOneWP Not to mention rumored to volunteer feeding old people and rescuing abandoned puppies

9:42pm

 KingofSlack@WiseOneWP But hey, you got a shot. Girls love the dorks who "volunteer" to try out the newest PlayStation.

9:42pm

 WiseOneWP@KingofSlack Whatever man. She and I have more in common. Does JD go to her horse shows?

9:45pm

 WiseOneWP@KingofSlack Or work on the school paper? Or read for that matter?

9:45pm

 WiseOneWP@KingofSlack I even wrote her a question to help with her column. Would JD do that?

9:45pm

 KingofSlack@WiseOneWP Prolly not. He has a life.

9:50pm

 KingofSlack@WiseOneWP I still can't believe you did that by the way.

9:50pm

 WiseOneWP@KingofSlack Whatever. She liked it! And the answer was good. You shouldn't wait outside. That's rude.

9:51pm

KingofSlack@WiseOneWP Bud, u r such a softy. And how would u know—your last date was freshman year with your cousin's friend.
9:52pm

 KingofSlack@WiseOneWP Who, if I recall, ditched u for another guy at the restaurant
9:52pm

 WiseOneWP@KingofSlack This coming from a guy whose dream girl attends Comic-Con
9:53pm

 KingofSlack@WiseOneWP Don't knock the alien chicks. They are wild. I g2g to do some homework. And u, my friend, need to move on.
9:55pm

 WiseOneWP@KingofSlack Just you wait and see . . . Claire will forget JD someday, guaranteed.
10:00pm

 KingofSlack@WiseOneWP Oh sure. I actually just read that pigs flew over a house the other day. Later Romeo.
10:01pm

 WiseOneWP Yeah, I thought I heard snorting but just figured you'd fallen asleep. Night.
10:31pm

Tuesday, March 16, 2010

AND SO IT BEGINS . . .

Spring semester is here, and now yours truly will be answering your most pressing questions—what is more fattening in the caf . . . the sloppy joes or the hash browns? (Do you really need to ask? Or want to know the answer? I'm guessing grease and fat have been spread equally among our caf's delights.) How do you ask out the prom queen if you are a shy newbie? (Strength be with you. You'll need bravery on your side.) What do you tell your parents when they walk in on you and your boy/girlfriend? (I have no freaking idea. I didn't even know you could get boys to come into your room.)

Now I'm sure you are asking yourself, why would I take advice from this random column? Or even more likely, WHO the heck is Get Clueless? And furthermore, why would someone who can only answer a third of her own questions decide to write an advice column?

I wish I could reassure you with a long list of appropriate qualifications, but the truth is, I can't. I've gone to Watkins Prep since I was in pre-K. I have absolutely no clue about love or life. I'm the kind of girl who reads other people's advice columns to get advice. If I were cast in a movie, I'd be the bumbling sidekick girl that people bet can't be made into the prom queen. But I'll give your questions my best shot. As my mom says, a fresh eye can be a wise eye.

So send your questions to me—at the paper's email or via my blog, GetClueless. I have a few already that I've answered to get the party started. Here's to being Clueless . . .

Dear Clueless,
Is it true that peanut butter can cure hickeys? My older sister told me that it was a surefire plan . . .
—All Marked Up

Dear All Marked Up,

I've had about as many hickeys as I've had shark encounters, scuffles with serial killers, Olympic gold medal performances, and vampire run-ins. Which is to say, none at all. Although I am a big fan of scarves, so I imagine that if I did find myself with a purple neck, I would go that route instead of reaching for the peanut butter.

However, if you are set on the nuttier method (pun intended), I would advise doing a "test patch" like they tell you to do when you use hair dye or home-waxing kits. I'd suggest not just globbing and going. You might get a bigger bite taken out if you stumble upon a particularly hungry soccer player. Or worse, your hickey giver could come back, and who knows? He or she might have a peanut allergy and explaining that one to an emergency room doctor is something I CAN'T help you with. No one, except maybe one of those vampires I haven't met, wants to risk being involved in a fatal neck-sucking session. And I'm guessing you are not a vampire. Or are you?

After careful consideration, I've decided on my final answer. Wear a scarf. Or a turtleneck. Or both. You will be fashionable and discreet.

We got this one from the blog I just started. You can GET CLUELESS anytime if you want. Check it out! (http://tiny.cc/GyGa5)

What is the appropriate first-date behavior— knock on the front door or wait outside and honk?
—Confused Dude at the Curb

Dear Confused,

Simple. You HAVE to knock and go inside. If you don't, the girl doesn't get her staircase moment. And EVERY girl wants a staircase moment.

That's it for today. It takes a lot out of a girl to help those in need. Or rather, to figure out answers to things she's never had to deal with. Ever. Keep the questions coming in and remember, even if you think you are clueless, you can't be worse off than me.

ClaireRBear Back from the barn and wasting time . . . why did I take on so much spring semester?
6:03pm

 ClaireRBear And who came up with trigonometry? Were they related to the devil? I think perhaps so.
6:05pm

 KingofSlack Parents on case about talking college apps. I'm on case about making perfect playlist.
6:05pm

 WiseOneWP They might have a point. *RT@KingofSlack Parents on case about talking college apps.*
6:07pm

 KingofSlack Didn't realize I had my own guidance counselor. *RT@WiseOneWP They might have a point.*
6:08pm

 ClaireRBear@KingofSlack He DOES have a point, my friend.
6:08pm

 KingofSlack would very much like his friends to leave him alone to work on his playlist. Ignoring tweets.
6:10pm

Lots0love@ClaireRBear Evening little lady. How goes it? Stressed I see.
6:23pm

 ClaireRBear@Lots0love You could say that. This column is killing me. And I have like 3 papers due at end of week.
6:24pm

ClaireRBear@Lots0love What's up with you? Any word from Fabrizio?
6:24pm

 Lots0love@ClaireRBear Fabrizio and I are dunzo I'm afraid. The distance was too great.
6:26pm

 Lots0love@ClaireRBear But I DID meet this new guy today when I was at the mall trying to find a cute new outfit to get me over Fab . . .
6:27pm

 ClaireRBear@Lots0love Why am I not surprised?
6:27pm

 Lots0love@ClaireRBear Bear, do you insinuate I'm forward?
6:30pm

 ClaireRBear@Lots0love Why no. I don't insinuate. It's a fact. :)
6:30pm

 KingofSlack If you had to choose between being a cyborg or a terminator, which would you choose?
6:30pm

 KingofSlack If you chose terminator, which version would you be—Arnold from first movie, or chick from third?
6:30pm

KingofSlack@ClaireRBear Yo. Which would you rather be?
6:31pm

 ClaireRBear@KingofSlack Jeez Benn. That's a question that's been keeping me up at night.
6:32pm

 KingofSlack Some people are just not visionaries.
6:35pm

 Lots0love@ClaireRBear UH, HELLO? Not cool to leave friend hanging for 10 minutes when new love to discuss.
6:40pm

 ClaireRBear@Lots0love Sorry! Benn sucked me into a quick debate on sci-fi. I'm back. So where'd you meet new love?
6:41pm

 Lots0love@ClaireRBear The rents dropped me off at Sandy Points after lax and I was just browsing the racks in Nordstrom.
6:41pm

 Lots0love@ClaireRBear And there was a guy wandering in the girls' section looking totally lost. So, being a kind shopper, I asked him if he needed help.
6:43pm

 Lots0love@ClaireRBear Turns out he was buying a birthday present for his sister. Isn't that sweet?
6:43pm

Lots0love@ClaireRBear Anyway, next thing I know we were chatting away and then we went and got some fro-yo in food court.

6:44pm

 Lots0love@ClaireRBear His name is Ford. Hot, right? He's a senior at Shore Hill Country Day.

6:44pm

 ClaireRBear@Lots0love You have a gift for meeting boys in the most random places.

6:45pm

 ClaireRBear@Lots0love Are you going to see Hot Name again then?

6:45pm

 Lots0love@ClaireRBear We have a date this Friday :) I have to go back to mall! I need to find a new cute 1st date outfit.

6:45pm

 ClaireRBear@Lots0love Again, this is why YOU should be writing column, not me.

6:47pm

 Lots0love@ClaireRBear You are doing great. Plus, you will find a guy soon, I'm sure of it. Like maybe JD. Just saying. :)

6:47pm

 ClaireRBear@Lots0love Please tell me you didn't?

6:47pm

 Lots0love@ClaireRBear Didn't what? Didn't happen to mention my super cute BFF who is like, super smart and funny and single?

6:48pm

ClaireRBear@Lots0love Charlotte May Matthews!
6:48pm

 Lots0love@ClaireRBear Calm down sweetie. You are so gullible. I didn't say anything. But I don't know why I shouldn't.
6:50pm

 Lots0love@ClaireRBear Or why YOU can't talk to him. He is always hanging with the lax girls and guys. And I'M a lax girl . . .
6:50pm

 ClaireRBear@Lots0love I couldn't. He is too perfect. Honestly, don't you remember what Jessica said? He was just nice to me cause he's generous like that.
6:51pm

 Lots0love@ClaireRBear She is a fool and that is not true. You are going to have to talk to him. I demand it.
6:59pm

 Lots0love@ClaireRBear Like you said, we are almost seniors and that means JD is almost outta here.
7:00pm

 ClaireRBear@Lots0love Yeah, yeah. Can we change the subject puh-lease?
7:07pm

 KingofSlack Bored and more bored. Tweeting again to save myself from boredom.
7:15pm

Lots0love@ClaireRBear Fine. But I'm just saying, maybe if you ever got out of the comp lab and away from Will & Benn . . . he'd see you.
7:16pm

 ClaireRBear@Lots0love Hey, leave the boys alone. They're all I got when you are off being Miss Popular.
7:20pm

 KingofSlack@ClaireRBear Who'd see you?
7:20pm

 Lots0love@ClaireRBear I told you freshman yr to try out for lax team and you chose horses instead. I tried.
7:24pm

 ClaireRBear@KingofSlack Nobody. Nothing. Forget it.
7:25pm

 ClaireRBear I sometimes wonder how I ended up with such random—and bigmouthed—friends.
7:30pm

 Lots0love Going to dins with moms and pops. Another night of hearing about my failings as a student.
7:31pm

 KingofSlack Will someone please save me from this tedium?
7:49pm

 ClaireRBear@KingofSlack Don't you have a video game you could play or a comic you could read?
8:02pm

KingofSlack@ClaireRBear For your information, my parents are restricting my game time. Apparently they read an article about it rotting the brain.
8:02pm

 KingofSlack@ClaireRBear And i've read all my comics thank u very much.
8:02pm

 KingofSlack@ClaireRBear Whatcha up to? Maybe I could come there and watch Battlestar.
8:10pm

 ClaireRBear@KingofSlack No can do my friend. Need to work. Go hang at Will's if you are so lonely.
8:15pm

 KingofSlack Everybody is boring. I'm out.
8:15pm

 ClaireRBear Crybaby. *RT@KingofSlack Everybody is boring. I'm out.*
8:20pm

WiseOneWP When will this neverending week come to an end?

Friday, March 19, 1:11pm

 KingofSlack New alien movie opens this weekend. Guaranteed to dominate box office!

1:23pm

 ClaireRBear Um, the week ends today. Duh. *RT@WiseOneWP When will this neverending week come to an end?*

2:33pm

 Lots0love DATE NIGHT!! Woo-hoo.

2:33pm

 KingofSlack Someone is in a rather foul mood. *RT@ClaireRBear Um, the week ends today. Duh.*

3:35pm

 ClaireRBear Someone is in danger of having a pencil thrown at him. *RT@KingofSlack Someone is in a rather foul mood.*

3:36pm

 WiseOneWP@ClaireRBear What's going on? If you hit the keyboard any harder you are going to break it.

3:40pm

 ClaireRBear Where to begin with what's wrong with this day?

3:40pm

 ClaireRBear A certain adviser had the nerve to criticize my advice. Said it didn't answer enough. It's CLUELESS!! That's the point!

3:40pm

ClaireRBear My dad was supposed to come to my horse show this weekend but apparently new wife needs him at some fund-raiser.

3:42pm

 ClaireRBear And apparently I'm invisible.

3:42pm

 WiseOneWP@ClaireRBear Oh. That's all? :)

3:45pm

 ClaireRBear@WiseOneWP I would laugh but can't. Too miserable.

3:45pm

 WiseOneWP@ClaireRBear Cheer up—at least you aren't Bennett. Check out his shirt . . .

3:46pm

 ClaireRBear@WiseOneWP LOL!! I didn't see that when he walked into comp lab! He's wearing a Team Speidi T-shirt for real?

3:48pm

 ClaireRBear@KingofSlack@WiseOneWP Nice shirt Benn. The ladies must be all over u :)

3:50pm

KingofSlack@ClaireRBear@WiseOneWP Don't hate y'all. Appreciate.
3:50pm

 ClaireRBear@KingofSlack@WiseOneWP Whatever you say big guy.
3:51pm

 ClaireRBear@WiseOneWP Thanks for trying to cheer me up but I think it is not in cards.
4:01pm

 WiseOneWP@ClaireRBear Well, if there is anything I can do, just let me know.
4:02pm

 ClaireRBear@WiseOneWP Not much you can do. Apparently I'm a hack writer, JD will NEVER notice me, and my dad doesn't even love me enough to ditch the new wife for one day.
4:03pm

 WiseOneWP@ClaireRBear NONE of that is true. Please try to smile—otherwise I'll have to look at Benn's stupid grin for rest of afternoon.
4:05pm

 ClaireRBear@WiseOneWP At least Lottie has a new guy which means she will distract me with tales of epic romance . . . until she decides he's no good. ·
4:09pm

45

WiseOneWP@ClaireRBear There is at least that.
4:12pm

 ClaireRBear I'm taking a break. I need fresh air.
4:16pm

 KingofSlack My friends don't think my wardrobe is cool. I think my friends aren't cool.
4:30pm

 Lots0love Just finished lacrosse practice. Time to start date practice!
4:31pm

BIG MOUTH B

What a boy wants, what a boy needs . . .
are two very different things.

Friday, March 19, 4:45pm

Spring is in the air. Cue the sound of chirping birds,
the image of blooming flowers, a cloudless blue sky
. . . or in my case, the incessant cawing of a crow,
the image of me sneezing due to wicked allergies,
and the beginnings of a farmer's tan as my lily-white
skin did not react kindly to the round of golf I played
after school yesterday. Thanks UV rays. Doing a fine
job.

Along with all these pleasant things, spring is also the
time (at least in movies and books) when LOVE is in
the air. That indescribable feeling that makes people
act goofy, spend money, and in many a case,
abandon their friends. I am very suspicious of this
thing called love. I do not trust an emotion that gives
people personality makeovers. Or makes guys start
believing that they actually LIKE Matthew
McConaughey movies. Dudes, you don't. Your
girlfriend or object of your current attention does.
YOU hate him because you will NEVER have abs
like him. Or a girlfriend/baby mama as hot as his.
Trust me.

My point is, love makes people do funny things, and I bring this up now because one of my friends has been suffering from a lovebug bite for too long. He has been under the false hope that love gives. I fear that, if he doesn't get a cure or a vaccine or even a push off the ledge he's been leaning over, he will never recover. Frankly, I would be shocked if he ever admitted his feelings to the person he is smitten with without some shoving . . . but stranger things have happened, I guess. I mean, I heard that there was a baby born with two sets of DNA because it actually "absorbed" its twin in the womb. Nope, wait, that was an episode of Fringe. So, no, stranger things have NOT happened.

I myself have very high standards when it comes to love. A girl must meet the stringent requirements below for me to even contemplate anything. This list is the result of a LOT of thinking and observing. Without further ado, my requirements for love:

- She has to be a girl (one who likes Syfy channel is preferred but not mandatory).
- She must be breathing.

That's it. Okay, maybe not so stringent. But hey, who are we kidding, I'm a guy. It doesn't take much.

I'm out for now, Prepsters. Enjoy the spring, but beware the lovebugs. I heard they leave a nasty mark.

ClaireRBear Back from break and still not feeling refreshed. Guess I can read through more clueless questions. That's a good way to kill time.
4:45pm

 Lots0love Preparation can fully begin. Wish I had figured out something to talk about before the big night!!
4:50pm

 KingofSlack Blog complete. Happy reading, followers.
4:52pm

 KingofSlack@WiseOneWP What's up with Claire? She is especially snippy today.
4:54pm

 WiseOneWP@KingofSlack Ease up. She's having a bad day. I hate when she gets so down and hard on herself.
4:54pm

 WiseOneWP@KingofSlack I wish I could cheer her up.
4:58pm

 KingofSlack@WiseOneWP You could get her a date with JD. That would probably work. Too bad you're not him.
4:58pm

 KingofSlack@WiseOneWP Holy frak! That's it!!! U CAN BE JD.
5:06pm

WiseOneWP@KingofSlack What are you talking about?

5:06pm

 KingofSlack@WiseOneWP This is exactly the push I was blogging about! Man I'm good.

5:07pm

 KingofSlack@WiseOneWP This is pure brilliance!! I'm a genius. Like, i should have my own show or movie or cult or something.

5:07pm

 WiseOneWP@KingofSlack Would you be so kind as to tell me WHAT YOU ARE TALKING ABOUT?

5:12pm

 KingofSlack@WiseOneWP Listen up my very unwise one. U just have to tweet Claire under a new name and when she asks who you are, say JD.

5:13pm

 KingofSlack@WiseOneWP Hold up. Just checked and the dude is without Twitter connections.

5:20pm

 WiseOneWP@KingofSlack Don't you think she would probably figure something is going on when JD doesn't talk to her at school?

5:21pm

 KingofSlack@WiseOneWP You are just going to send her one message. To give her something to smile about. Then u drop it. No harm, no foul.

5:23pm

KingofSlack@WiseOneWP See? Genius! And added bonus: when "JD" doesn't tweet again, you'll be there to comfort. U got nice shoulders, bud.

5:23pm

 KingofSlack@WiseOneWP Another bonus: you'll get risk-free flirting practice with Claire. For someone as smitten as u r, u don't do nearly enough of that.

5:24pm

 WiseOneWP@KingofSlack I don't know about this

5:24pm

 KingofSlack@WiseOneWP Claire is screaming for help, dude. Seriously. Like she's literally screaming and it is giving me a headache.

5:25pm

 KingofSlack@WiseOneWP Please just send her a tweet. Please. I think she might actually break a computer monitor.

5:26pm

 WiseOneWP@KingofSlack You want me to make a new profile and send her one tweet as Jack Dyson. That's it? Then I go on my merry way and she goes on hers?

5:26pm

 WiseOneWP@KingofSlack Thinking the whole time that her killer crush, the love of her life, actually sought her out?

5:26pm

KingofSlack@WiseOneWP See? Simple.

5:30pm

 KingofSlack@WiseOneWP She will be happy. You will be happy. I won't have to listen to you two complain. Win-win. And win.

5:30pm

 WiseOneWP@KingofSlack What would I even say to her??? She's gonna know it's me as soon as I write anything.

5:35pm

 KingofSlack@WiseOneWP IDK. Tell her you like rabbits.

5:35pm

 WiseOneWP@KingofSlack That is mind-blowingly lame.

5:37pm

 KingofSlack@WiseOneWP So? As the dreamy Jack Dyson, nothing you do or say could possibly be lame.

5:38pm

 WiseOneWP@KingofSlack He isn't THAT great. Jeez. You really think it will make Claire smile?

5:41pm

 KingofSlack@WiseOneWP Hmmm . . . Is Star Wars a masterpiece?

5:43pm

 WiseOneWP@KingofSlack Good point. Let me think about it.

5:43pm

KingofSlack@WiseOneWP I think I can hear your heart pounding from over here . . . Get a grip. It's just Claire

5:50pm

 WiseOneWP@KingofSlack It's never, ever, just Claire.

5:56pm

 Lots0love Date due to arrive any minute. Hair—check. Killer outfit—check. Witty remarks—check. This is in the bag!

7:23pm

 ClaireRBear Have fun. At least one of us is getting out.

7:30pm

 ClaireRBear Two choices—homework or tv. Such a difficult decision.

7:30pm

 Lots0love@ClaireRBear Hang out with the boys. It's Friday. I'm sure they got nothing going on.

7:31pm

 KingofSlack I resent that implication. *RT@Lots0love It's Friday. I'm sure they got nothing going on*

7:32pm

 Lots0love@KingofSlack The truth can hurt, can't it?

7:35pm

53

WiseOneWP@KingofSlack Okay, I think I'm going to do it.
7:40pm

 KingofSlack@WiseOneWP Watch a marathon of Transporter movies with me? Nice!
7:46pm

 WiseOneWP@KingofSlack Yup. Exactly. OR, I'm going to send Claire a message. As JD.
7:50pm

 KingofSlack@WiseOneWP Wise choice, WiseOne.
7:51pm

 WiseOneWP@KingofSlack You really think so? It doesn't feel very wise.
7:51pm

 KingofSlack@WiseOneWP What could happen? U are only going to send her one message. I'm pretty sure the world will continue to rotate on its axis
7:52pm

 KingofSlack@WiseOneWP Although, if it doesn't, that would be cool too. Maybe we'd find an alternate universe.
7:53pm

 KingofSlack@WiseOneWP And in said universe, maybe u really ARE JD! Like a cool version of u.
7:53pm

 WiseOneWP@KingofSlack PLEASE FOCUS! Okay, you've got my back, right?
7:54pm

KingofSlack@WiseOneWP Always. Go forth and tweet. Claire will be happy. You will be happy. And then we can watch Transporter.

7:55pm

 WiseOneWP@KingofSlack Fine. If this comes back to bite me . . .

7:55pm

 KingofSlack@WiseOneWP It WON'T. Stop whining and start tweeting. Good luck, Casanova.

7:56pm

ClaireRBear Want to hear what happened on friend's big date!
8:37pm

 KingofSlack Friday night. No plans. Except for shoving someone.
8:37pm

TopofGame17 is now following **ClaireRBear**
8:40pm

 KingofSlack@ClaireRBear What big date? Lottie got a new boyfriend?
8:48pm

 ClaireRBear@KingofSlack What are u doing still tweeting? No hot dates with Stargate? And yup, Lottie's in love again.
8:50pm

 KingofSlack@ClaireRBear Where does she find the time? I think she discovered a loop in the time/space continuum and has 27-hour days.
8:52pm

 ClaireRBear@KingofSlack Of course YOU would think that.
8:53pm

 KingofSlack@ClaireRBear U wish u were as smart. JK. Will and I are coming to your show Sunday u know.
9:02pm

ClaireRBear@KingofSlack Cool. Just try not to scare the horses this time by wearing that alien hat . . .
9:10pm

 KingofSlack@ClaireRBear I can't promise . . .
9:15pm

 TopofGame17@ClaireRBear This Clueless chick?
9:17pm

 KingofSlack@ClaireRBear It's not the hat. You know Will cannot get the "golfer" clap down. It is two fingers lightly tapping . . . I'll talk to him.
9:17pm

 ClaireRBear@KingofSlack You do that. Hey—you know someone named TopofGame17??
9:20pm

 KingofSlack@ClaireRBear Uh, nope. Not that I recall. g2g.
9:31pm

 ClaireRBear@KingofSlack Okay then, Mr. Hot Then Cold. Have fun doing whatever.
9:32pm

 ClaireRBear@TopofGame17 This is Clueless. Mr. Schaberg, is that you?
9:34pm

TopofGame17@ClaireRBear Not the teach. Just a fan. A guy in my history class told me this was your Twitter name. Wanted to tell you I liked the column . . .
9:35pm

 ClaireRBear@TopofGame17 Um, thank you! You should tell that to Mr. Schaberg.
9:35pm

 TopofGame17@ClaireRBear Maybe I will! U r great. Loved the hickey one—will have to try that trick on my little brother some time
9:40pm

 ClaireRBear@TopofGame17 Ha! I can't believe someone asked that question. I bet it was my friend Bennett.
9:41pm

 TopofGame17@ClaireRBear The other ones were good too—the date one. What's a staircase moment?
9:45pm

 ClaireRBear@TopofGame17 It's silly. It's when a girl shows up and a guy suddenly realizes she is beautiful—usually occurs at the top of a staircase.
9:47pm

 TopofGame17@ClaireRBear Ah!! Got it! Like in My Fair Lady.
9:50pm

 ClaireRBear@TopofGame17 EXACTLY! Or in the oh so intellectual Not Just Another Teen Movie.
9:51pm

TopofGame17@ClaireRBear Or Gone with the Wind . . .
9:51pm

 ClaireRBear@TopofGame17 Fan of the old-school films I see . . .
9:57pm

 TopofGame17@ClaireRBear I like to think I'm multifaceted. Keep up good work. U got me laughing.
10:00pm

 ClaireRBear@TopofGame17 Will do—hey, who are you by the way? Not really a dog, Ipresume?
10:01pm

 TopofGame17@ClaireRBear Oh sorry. Forgot that you don't always know real names on this thing. Keep my profile blank. I'm JD Whitcomb. Have a good night.
10:13pm

 ClaireRBear@TopofGame17 Oh. Hey. I'm Claire. I ride with your sister. So yeah, night.
10:13pm

 ClaireRBear@Lots0love Is someone playing a trick on me? For real, universe is messing with me.
10:14pm

WiseOneWP@KingofSlack I just did it!! Holy crap. It felt intensely weird, but I'm pretty sure Claire was suprised in a good way.

10:17pm

KingofSlack@WiseOneWP I take it you are TopofGame17? Claire asked me if I knew you.

10:20pm

WiseOneWP@KingofSlack That would be me—or JD, I guess. Are you going to IHOP tmrw morning? Come by after.

10:28pm

KingofSlack@WiseOneWP After I'm fully stuffed with stuffed waffles, I'll swing by. Keep up the good work my boy. You can't go wrong if u stick to plan.

10:28pm

KingofSlack@WiseOneWP One time tweet. Then radio silence. Silence is golden, remember?

10:31pm

WiseOneWP@KingofSlack Um, yeah sure. Silence. Golden. Got it.

11:13pm

Lots0love It's Friday and I'm in love . . .
Saturday, March 20 1:15pm

KingofSlack@Lots0love Hey genius—it's not Friday. Coming to Claire's show tmrw?
1:17pm

Lots0love@KingofSlack Hey dork—I know. Was quoting a song which you would know if you listened to anything but Lord of Rings soundtrack.
1:24pm

KingofSlack@Lots0love mori er
1:31pm

Lots0love@KingofSlack Say what? Are you throwing crazy made-up languages at me again?
1:40pm

KingofSlack@Lots0love Glad u don't speak Elvish. U don't want to know what I just called u.
1:40pm

Lots0love@KingofSlack I cannot understand why Claire hangs out with you.
1:41pm

KingofSlack@Lots0love Simple. I'm a stud muffin.
1:42pm

Lots0love@KingofSlack Muffin maybe. Stud, not so much.
1:42pm

KingofSlack@Lots0love Speaking of stud . . . how was the big date?

1:50pm

 Lots0love@KingofSlack None of your business. Now, if you will excuse me, going to talk to my real friend . . .

1:55pm

 KingofSlack Me doth think she protesteth too mucheth . . .

1:55pm

 Lots0love@KingofSlack The lady doth protest too much, methinks. Sorry, but I can't bear to hear you mistweet my boy Will Shakes.

1:56pm

 KingofSlack@Lots0love Remind me again why you claim to be cooler than me?

1:56pm

 Lots0love@KingofSlack I don't claim. I am.

1:57pm

 Lots0love@ClaireRBear Hello lovely. Have you left for barn yet? Want to hear about my new and lasting love?

1:58pm

 Lots0love@ClaireRBear He looks like this picture . . .

1:58pm

 ClaireRBear@Lots0love LOL! I didn't know you were dating reality stars now!

2:02pm

Lots0love@ClaireRBear Well, he might as well be. He is SO cute! And we had so much fun last night. Emma and Harris almost caught us.
2:05pm

 ClaireRBear@Lots0love Caught you?
2:05pm

 Lots0love@ClaireRBear Erm, yeah, as in caught us making out.
2:08pm

 ClaireRBear@Lots0love Riiight! Hey, I have to live up to my column title, right?
2:08pm

 Lots0love@ClaireRBear No no! Fair question. I was being vague.
2:09pm

 Lots0love@ClaireRBear Anyway, he is an AMAZING kisser. Not too wet, not too much tongue. Think this one has potential!
2:09pm

 ClaireRBear@Lots0love Of course you do. That's great, L.
2:11pm

 ClaireRBear@Lots0love Um . . . so . . . I have something to tell you, too.
2:15pm

 Lots0love@ClaireRBear What's going on?
2:20pm

ClaireRBear@Lots0love JD Whitcomb sent me a message on Twitter last night!!

2:20pm

 ClaireRBear@Lots0love Hello?

2:26pm

 Lots0love@ClaireRBear I'm sorry! Had to give myself Heimlich. Did you say JD sent you a tweet??

2:26pm

 ClaireRBear@Lots0love Insane, right? He was pretty nice actually.

2:26pm

 Lots0love@ClaireRBear Nice actually?? You have wanted this to happen since you knew there was something besides horses in this world.

2:27pm

 Lots0love@ClaireRBear How can you be so calm!?! I can't believe I'M more excited than you!

2:28pm

 ClaireRBear@Lots0love LOL! I'm not going to get that excited yet. It was just a few tweets. I'm sure I'll never hear from him again.

2:30pm

 ClaireRBear@Lots0love But have to admit, it was pretty cool.

2:30pm

Lots0love@ClaireRBear I would certainly think so my Bear!! Yeah! Emma is calling. You will have to tell me more tmrw after show.
2:30pm

 Lots0love@ClaireRBear Break a leg! xoxo
2:34pm

 KingofSlack Who is breaking whose leg? Has the mafia come to South Carolina?
2:45pm

ClaireRBear Another weekend over, another horse-show down. Might actually qualify for finals early this year. Go, Maverick!

Monday, March 22, 12:10pm

 ClaireRBear Mom was at it again!

12:11pm

 Lots0love@ClaireBear Caught her emailing with her secret lovah? *RT@ClaireRBear Mom was at it again!*

12:15pm

 ClaireRBear YES! My mother has a boyfriend! Why else would she always shut the door in my face when I try to come into computer room?

12:15pm

 ClaireRBear Or maybe she is addicted to solitaire and is ashamed for me to know? Or gambles online?

12:20pm

 ClaireRBear Or all of the above? Maybe I'll never know.

12:21pm

 KingofSlack@ClaireRBear Congrats on the big win. It was all b/c I brought Maverick his super special treat.

12:21pm

 ClaireRBear@KingofSlack You mean the cinnamon sugar bagel that gave my horse the hiccups . . . That treat?

12:25pm

 KingofSlack@ClaireRBear It worked didn't it? U were so freaked out he was going to hiccup whole time u didn't get nervous.

12:25pm

KingofSlack@ClaireRBear Will's face was priceless when Mav had that first hiccup.
12:26pm

 ClaireRBear@KingofSlack It was pretty funny! I'm glad you guys came out. You even played nice with Lottie. Mom was happy to see you as per usual
12:31pm

 ClaireRBear@KingofSlack Swear to God, she wants to adopt you and Will. No idea why . . .
12:33pm

 KingofSlack@ClaireRBear B/c we both know how to appreciate the ladies.
12:35pm

 ClaireRBear@KingofSlack Ew. Gross!
12:35pm

 KingofSlack@ClaireRBear Somebody seems to be in an awfully good mood 2day . . . u going to still be nice at paper mtg later?
12:35pm

Lots0love@ClaireRBear Mucho congrats darling. You looked like a star. You still floating on a cloud?
12:40pm

 ClaireRBear@Lots0love The cloud is still there but slightly dark. Can't believe Dad really blew the show off!
12:41pm

 ClaireRBear@Lots0love I bet it was because the peroxide blonde was worried she'd get mud on her Jimmy Choos.
12:42pm

 Lots0love@ClaireRBear Or mayybe she was worried a horse would mistake her for a really big carrot with that tan in a can she's rocking.
12:43pm

 ClaireRBear@Lots0love Exactly! I just don't get my dad. It's like he's completely forgotten I exist. At all.
12:44pm

 Lots0love@ClaireRBear I'm sorry. He sucks. So does the step-witch. But on the plus side—JD tweeted you :)
12:45pm

 ClaireRBear@Lots0love That does add a silver lining to my cloud.
12:45pm

 Lots0love@ClaireRBear So did you share your big news with him????
12:46pm

 ClaireRBear@Lots0love No! Are you crazy? Why would I do that??
12:46pm

Lots0love@ClaireRBear Um, I don't know. Because you LIKE him. Wasn't his sister at the show? You could just say hi and that she did a good job.

12:46pm

 ClaireRBear@Lots0love That's so . . . forward. I'm not that kind of girl.

12:47pm

 Lots0love@ClaireRBear Buck up sister. It won't kill you. Just do what I said. Trust me. Guys like girls who aren't all damsel in distressy.

12:47pm

 ClaireRBear@Lots0love That isn't even a word.

12:47pm

 Lots0love@ClaireRBear Enough dilly-dallying. Don't make me find you in the library and force you to type.

12:48pm

 ClaireRBear@Lots0love Okay, okay. Jeez you can be a bully!

12:49pm

 Lots0love@ClaireRBear But you love me anyway. Good luck lady. See you after school!

12:50pm

ClaireRBear@TopofGame17 Hey, saw your sister at the show this weekend. She did really well!

4:05pm

 ClaireRBear@TopofGame17 She and I ride together. At Gunnery Stables?

4:06pm

 TopofGame17@ClaireRBear Hi. Oh, right! I forgot you ride. Impressive . . . horses scare me.

4:16pm

 ClaireRBear@TopofGame17 Been riding forever. Love it. I'm surprised you would be scared by a little old horse. No worries, my friend Will is too . . .

4:18pm

 TopofGame17@ClaireRBear Can see why. Those things are huge. Nothing little about them.

4:19pm

 ClaireRBear@TopofGame17 So I take it you are more comfortable with the lax stick and field . . .

4:20pm

 TopofGame17@ClaireRBear Oh, yeah, I mean, I guess. Don't get me wrong, love animals.

4:22pm

 ClaireRBear@TopofGame17 I take it that explains choice of profile pic? Would have thought you'd go for a bulldog—cause Watkins Prep Dawgs. Is that one yours?

4:23pm

 TopofGame17@ClaireRBear What? Oh, guess I could have gone with a bulldog. Just like boxers. Think they get a bad rep. Big softies. Want to get one someday.

4:24pm

ClaireRBear@TopofGame17 HA!
4:25pm

 TopofGame17@ClaireRBear What's so funny?
4:27pm

 ClaireRBear@TopofGame17 Nothing really. Just that I heard a rumor that you feed homeless pets and stuff. Thought it wasn't true. Maybe I was wrong.
4:30pm

 TopofGame17@ClaireRBear Oh. Yeah, um. I did that once. Rumor not entirely false.
4:35pm

 ClaireRBear@TopofGame17 Well, it is only fitting that JD Whitcomb would be kind to animals.
4:36pm

 TopofGame17@ClaireRBear What is that supposed to mean?
4:36pm

 ClaireRBear@TopofGame17 Nothing. I should get going. Talk later?
4:41pm

 ClaireRBear@TopofGame17 Maybe I'll see u in the hallways . . .
4:41pm

 TopofGame17@ClaireRBear Yeah, maybe.
4:42pm

WiseOneWP Is it a requirement that Mondays always be long and usually horrible?
6:32pm

 ClaireRBear Home early. Never sure what to do when not riding.
6:32pm

 ClaireRBear Problem solved. Law & Order on. SVU is the best.
6:33pm

 WiseOneWP Or are there other factors at work on this particular day?
6:33pm

 WiseOneWP@KingofSlack Dude! Claire tweeted me!!
6:35pm

 KingofSlack@WiseOneWP And your point would be?
6:36pm

 WiseOneWP@KingofSlack She tweeted me—as JD!! Now do you see the point?
6:40pm

 KingofSlack@WiseOneWP Well you didn't answer right? Because that would not be sticking to the plan. You answered her, didn't you? Why would u do that?
6:43pm

WiseOneWP@KingofSlack No excuse. When I saw her this morning she was super happy about tweets this weekend. Didn't want to leave her hanging.
6:47pm

 WiseOneWP@KingofSlack She is going to kill me if she finds out.
6:50pm

 KingofSlack@WiseOneWP No kidding. So she can't. Stop now while u r ahead.
6:55pm

 WiseOneWP@KingofSlack Easier said than done. It's like she WANTED to rub it in
6:58pm

 KingofSlack@WiseOneWP Oh, yeah. I'm sure. She totally knows u pretended to be her crush and now wants to make u feel guilty. Totally.
7:01 pm

 WiseOneWP@KingofSlack Point taken.
7:01pm

 KingofSlack@WiseOneWP It better be my friend. I don't want to be the one picking up the pieces after she throws you in the shredder.
7:08pm

 WiseOneWP@KingofSlack I said POINT TAKEN!
7:10pm

ClaireRBear Have a whole week off from riding—gotta give my boy some time to recuperate. Too bad paper isn't giving me the same break.

7:35pm

 Lots0love How will I last another four days without Ford?

7:35pm

 KingofSlack Holla! All three Lord of Rings back-2-back nights on TNT! Gotta love cable.

7:46pm

 KingofSlack@ClaireRBear@WiseOneWP U guys notice Mr. Schaberg's fly was open ALL day?? Dude— nothing I want to see!

7:46pm

 ClaireRBear@KingofSlack@WiseOneWP Are you for real?? So glad you didn't say anything while he was in room. EW!!

7:48pm

 KingofSlack@ClaireRBear@WiseOneWP Maybe if someone hadn't been so busy giggling with her friend over Twitter, she would have noticed.

7:49pm

 ClaireRBear@KingofSlack@WiseOneWP Jealous I wasn't paying attention to you, Benny? Some things a girl can share only with her girlfriends.

7:53pm

KingofSlack@ClaireRBear@WiseOneWP Let me guess—you and Lottie were giggling about Lottie's new boy?

7:53pm

 ClaireRBear@KingofSlack@WiseOneWP Why do you assume it was about a boy and Lottie? What if it was about me and a boy?

7:54pm

 KingofSlack@ClaireRBear@WiseOneWP B/c the only boys besides me and Will that you hang out with have four legs and a mane and tail.

7:56pm

 ClaireRBear@KingofSlack@WiseOneWP Bennett Jones you are a mean person who I should not call friend.

8:30pm

 WiseOneWP@ClaireRBear Ignore him—you know Benn can't take anything seriously.

8:31pm

 ClaireRBear@WiseOneWP Oh, I know. I've been friends with him for too long to really believe him when he is being mean.

8:31pm

 WiseOneWP@ClaireRBear Yeah, deep down he's a good guy—you just have to ignore his tendency to wear elf ears and speak in tongues.

8:31pm

KingofSlack The marathon is about to start. I don't need friends when I have orcs and hobbits to entertain me.

8:34pm

 ClaireRBear@WiseOneWP True. So guess what?? JD tweeted me the other day!! Can you believe it? I mean, you and I were JUST talking about him!

8:39pm

 ClaireRBear@WiseOneWP It wasn't really a long convo or anything but it was JD! He read my column! We've tweeted twice at this point.

8:39pm

 ClaireRBear@WiseOneWP Not that I'm counting or anything.

8:40pm

 ClaireRBear@WiseOneWP Probably nothing, but that kind of thing never happens to me.

8:45pm

 WiseOneWP@ClaireRBear Uh, cool. Well good for you.

8:47pm

 ClaireRBear@WiseOneWP Thanks for listening Will. I'm sure it's not that exciting for you.

8:50pm

 ClaireRBear@WiseOneWP It's nice . . . tweeting with you means I keep my mind off hoping to hear from him again.

8:51pm

WiseOneWP@ClaireRBear Sure, yeah, I get it. Glad I could help. Have a good night Claire.
8:53pm

 Lots0love Do I finish up homework now? Or wait till study hall? Thought of the day . . .
9:00pm

 KingofSlack Why bother with any other channels? I have enough drama in the real world. Give me fantasy TV any day.
9:14pm

KingofSlack Had to send this on. Woo-hoo! *RT@gamesrus New War Space coming to multi-platforms soon!*

Tuesday, March 23, 7:09am

 Lots0love Curse of living in the South: when the sun isn't shining, even more gloomy. Go away, gray skies.

7:10am

 ClaireRBear@WiseOneWP Please don't say anything to Benn about what I told you last night! I can't handle the teasing. Especially when JD never talks to me again.

7:13am

 WiseOneWP@ClaireRBear Why so sure you'll get the silent treatment?

7:15am

 ClaireRBear@WiseOneWP He sounded a little cagey when I said "talk later"

7:18am

 WiseOneWP@ClaireRBear Cagey? Over tweets? Isn't it hard to tell?

7:19am

 ClaireRBear@WiseOneWP I just know. He wasn't super enthusiastic. Probably for the best anyway. If he gets to know me, he'll realize I'm a dork.

7:23am

 ClaireRBear@WiseOneWP Rather just have that one moment and believe he might have thought I was cool for a second.

7:24am

WiseOneWP@ClaireRBear What are you talking about? You rock. Trust me. You should know that.
7:25am

 ClaireRBear@WiseOneWP Thanks. But you just think that b/c you're my friend. It's not the same thing. No offense.
7:26am

 WiseOneWP@ClaireRBear None taken. Well, for what its worth, I think JD would be lucky to go out with you
7:29am

 ClaireRBear@WiseOneWP You know what's weird? You and I never really talk like this in person . . .
7:31pm

 WiseOneWP@ClaireRBear That's probably b/c Benn is always there being Benn. Hard to be serious when he's imitating cyborgs or reenacting the Matrix slo-mo scene.
7:32am

 ClaireRBear@WiseOneWP Good point. Well, I like it. You're a good listener. I'm glad we're friends.
7:36am

 WiseOneWP@ClaireRBear Yeah, me too.
7:37am

 WiseOneWP@ClaireRBear Hey, we are probably doing a Battlestar marathon or Halo game tonight. Swing by if you get bored.
7:37am

ClaireRBear@WiseOneWP Thx for invite but I'm heading over to Lottie's for dinner. Taco night at the Matthews. Next time. Bye!

7:40am

 Lots0love Despite the rainy skies, I'm going to find the silver lining—I get to wear my fab new galoshes.

7:41am

 ClaireRBear So early and yet, feel like the day should be over. This is what I get for tossing and turning all night. School will be tough.

7:42am

 WiseOneWP@KingofSlack Dude, you gotta come over tonight. This is insane. I can't stop now . . . not yet.

7:42am

 WiseOneWP@KingofSlack We will discuss when you come over.

7:45am

 ClaireRBear Taco night is a no-go! Friend is ditching me for a date. Plan B?

4:38pm

ClaireRBear@WiseOneWP Taking you up on the offer of downtime with Halo. Be over around 6:20. Get your game on!

5:02pm

 KingofSlack@WiseOneWP Ooh la la. Shall I stay home and let you two have some QT?

5:04pm

 WiseOneWP@KingofSlack Don't even think about it Benn. Be there. I mean it.

5:10pm

 KingofSlack Due to unnecessary threats, I'm boycotting my friend's house. Just try to have fun without me.

6:30pm

WATKINS WEEKLY

Tuesday, March 23, 2010

WELL, SINCE YOU ASKED . . .

Once again, brought to you by the most clueless girl in Carolina, here are some questions that are in need of answering. I assume they're desperate, as people are writing to *me* to ask. And while we are on this topic, thanks for all the questions sent to my own page. I am horrible with technology. Gigabyte sounds like a prehistoric shark to me. So if I'm slow in responding, please excuse me.

> **Dear G.C.,**
> **Do you know the health center's policy on confidentiality?**
>
> **—Just Wondering**

Dear Just Wondering,

Do you really mean Just Wondering? Or do you mean, "Hypothetically, if my *friend* had something he needed checked out, but wanted to make sure his parents didn't find out anything about it, would the health center be a good place to go?" Am I right?

Listen, I have no idea what is wrong with you. I'm not a doctor. But I *am* guessing that if you want confidentiality, whatever you have is no good, and quite possibly icky. Look at that! There is one perk to being as socially stunted as I am— no health worries.

There is a little thing called doctor/patient confidentiality. I suggest going to the family doc. You should be fine. I hope.

Dear Clueless,
I have a *friend* who is always making plans and then breaking them. Do I call him out on it?
—Stood Up

Dear Stood Up,

I'm not good with confrontation. But if it bothers you, my answer is yes.

From: **ClaireBearR16@gmail.com**
Sent: Wednesday, March 24, 9:37pm
To: LottieM17@gmail.com
Subject: What a wild, wild life . . .

Hey darling,

How was Ford? Worth ditching me for?

I ended up going over to Will's house. Bennett was supposed to hang out too but bailed. He can be such a flake sometimes. And a wuss. Apparently he had a stomachache. Anyway, it was fine. For all the time the three of us spend together, I don't ever get a chance to hang out with just Will. And I know, you don't want to hear that he's cool, but he is. And sensitive (had a minor breakdown about dad which he handled). And funny. And not all that ugly. I might even say, cute. It is just an observation. I'm mean he's no JD. . . .

Speaking of, I haven't heard from him again. Not a peep. And it was weird b/c I passed him in the hall today on my way to chemistry and he didn't even notice me. I mean, he was talking to one of his lax guys but still, I would have maybe at least thought he would have said hi or smiled.

Okay, I HAVE to stop dwelling on this! Like I told

Will, it is probably nothing and I'm making a mountain out of a molehill as my mother would say. Speaking of my mother, if she doesn't fess up to the clandestine online love affair she is having, or whatever it is that keeps her in the den for hours, I'm going to have an intervention. Just you watch me.

Air-kisses!!!

From: **ParkerWill.2010@gmail.com**

Sent: Wednesday, March 24, 10:22pm

To: BennettJonesEsq@gmail.com

Subject: Thanks a lot buddy

Hey dude, hello?? Where were you?! You say you are going to come over. Claire says she isn't going to come over. Then you try to play matchmaker, she ends up at my house and you are nowhere to be found. Not cool, my friend.

I was a total nutcase. I'm sure she thinks I've got Asperger's or something. I couldn't really form sentences and I kept trying to avoid the topic of JD but she kept bringing him up. And then she cried! Not about JD. About her dad. Still, I had no idea what to do.

Clearly this was a horrible plan as she is like, head over heels in love with the idea of JD tweeting. How am I supposed to leave her hanging?

—Will

From: **LottieM17@gmail.com**
Sent: Thursday, March 25, 1:02am
To: ClaireBearR16@gmail.com
Subject: Re: What a wild, wild life . . .

Dearest Claire,

If you would be so kind as to refrain from overuse of exclamation points and capitalization at this moment, it would be greatly appreciated. My head is rather fuzzy and my eyes are kind of crossing. Emma and Harris had one of their Infamous impromptu dinner parties and yours truly was given the task of serving the hoi polloi their wine after arriving home from from a date. And I MAY have stolen a sip or two from the bottle. I know you are giving me the stink eye right now.

I will most definitely give your situation deeper thought when I'm in a clearer state of mind. At this time, I must leave you.

Nighty-night, future Mrs. JD Whitcomb!

From: **LottieM17@gmail.com**
Sent: Thursday, March 25, 9:05am
To: ClaireBearR16@gmail.com
Subject: Re: What a wild, wild life . . .

Wow! That email last night was remarkably coherent given the circumstances. Being at school makes my head hurt.

Everything hurts.

Listen, I want you to stop thinking so negatively. Remember, it's all about the power of positive thinking. How do you think I got over my hangover so quickly? Well, okay, that might be a bit of a lie . . . I feel like crap, but hey, I'm sure IF I thought positively it would go away.

My head still hurts. And I have the sinking feeling I might have drunk-texted Ford last night. Kind of glad I'm in class and can't check my phone . . . I'm going to go back to sleeping on my desk. I want to die.

Remind me how horrible I felt next time I volunteer for one of Emma and Harris's parties.

PS: Wannabes are coming to town Sunday!!! Can you come??? Pleeeaase! We haven't been to a concert in ages (and NO—Britney does not count as we can't tell anyone we went!)

PPS: Wait—Will?? You talked to Will about JD? I'm so confused. Does he actually speak without Bennett around?

PPPS: No matter what you say, I'm always going to think he's a dork. Sorry.

From: **ClaireBearR16@gmail.com**
Sent: Thursday, March 25, 10:30am
To: LottieM17@gmail.com
Subject: I love my best friend

Thanks deario. You are kind to be so positive. I will channel you as best I can.

I'm glad to hear that despite your naughty behavior, you are beginning to make a recovery—sort of. Although I imagine that you feel worse due to texting Ford than due to beverage choice. Am I right? Thank God I don't have JD's phone number! Can you imagine what disasters that would cause? I mean, one form of communication has already made me mental.

Let me know as soon as you find out what you said to Ford. I'm sure it was cute and sweet and he probably likes you even more now. Feel better!

xoxo

PS: Wannabes!?! Woo-hoo! It's on.
PPS: Why are you always so down on Will? He's a nice guy. There is nothing wrong with dorks. I'M a dork, remember?

From: **ClaireBearR16@gmail.com**
Sent: Thursday, March 25, 5:02pm
To: LottieM17@gmail.com
Subject: Re: I love my best friend

GUESS WHAT!?! JD touched me. I mean, I'm not sure if it was a flirty touch or just a touch, but today in the Student Center, I was a total klutz and almost tripped going up the stairs and he was going down the stairs and then he reached out to steady me and smiled. I mean, It happened over like two point five seconds. But still!! Maybe you were right. Maybe this could work out! If I were a singer, I'd sing right now. Don't laugh. I said "if."

xoxo

ClaireRBear Friend has abandoned me to go to bed, but I'm too wired to sleep.
Thursday, March 25, 9:06pm

 ClaireRBear Need to get my mind on something other than what it is on . . . A book maybe?
9:06pm

 ClaireRBear #Whattoread? Something old—Twelfth Night? Something new—Half-Life of Planets? Something borrowed, Emma? Something blue?
9:10pm

 ClaireRBear Wish that we still lived in the "big house." The barn was right out back and late at night when I wasn't tired, I'd go and read in my pony's stall.
9:15pm

 ClaireRBear Miss the crickets too. And the smell of hay. Here always steamy with occasional whiff of smoke from a fireplace b/c everyone has fires if it drops below sixty.
9:15pm

 KingofSlack It seems ClaireBear is feeling all sorts of poetic tonight.
9:31pm

 ClaireRBear maybe b/c someone is having a good week. *RT@KingofSlack It seems ClaireBear is feeling all sorts of poetic tonight.*
9:32pm

 KingofSlack Knows not to mess with his girl when she is poetic. Dreams sound like they'll be sweet. I hope I dream up new game codes for Halo.
9:40pm

ClaireRBear Still want to know **#Whattoread?** But I've decided on a stormy night like tonight more comforting to go with old familiars—or early bedtime.
9:43pm

 ClaireRBear@TopofGame17 Hey, just wanted to say thanks.
9:45pm

 TopofGame17@ClaireRBear Uh, you're welcome? What r u thxing me 4?
9:47pm

 ClaireRBear@TopofGame17 Helping me on the stairs in StuCe today. I could have totally bitten it.
9:50pm

 TopofGame17@ClaireRBear Oh right, that! No big deal. Just being a gentleman.
9:55pm

 ClaireRBear@TopofGame17 Have to admit, I was a bit surprised. Thought of you more as an officer than a gentleman . . .
9:55pm

 TopofGame17@ClaireRBear That makes no sense!
10:00pm

 ClaireRBear@TopofGame17 I know! I don't know what is wrong with me. I am capable of sounding smart with other friends.
10:04pm

TopofGame17@ClaireRBear oh, so we're friends now? Like you and that tall guy you always hang out with?

10:10pm

 ClaireRBear@TopofGame17 You mean Will Parker? He's one of my good friends. Nothing more.

10:11pm

 TopofGame17@ClaireRBear Gotcha. Well, if we are friends I should be honest with you. I'm not so big on this Twitter thing.

10:22pm

 ClaireRBear@TopofGame17 No? Why not? You mean like in general or just tweeting me?

10:25pm

 TopofGame17@ClaireRBear It's nothing personal. You are gr8. Just realized tweeting isn't my thing.

10:26pm

 TopofGame17@ClaireRBear Hope this doesn't feel like out of left field but when I tweeted, didn't think we'd end up chatting so much. I'm better in person.

10:27pm

 ClaireRBear@TopofGame17 Okay. Um, I guess that makes sense. Well, I'm glad we got to chat a little. Maybe next time in person?

10:30pm

ClaireRBear Time to sleep for real. Hoping for sweet dreams but doubting it.
10:41pm

 KingofSlack@ClaireRBear I'm awake! You could talk to me if you are bored
10:43pm

 ClaireRBear@KingofSlack I said I wanted sweet dreams, not dreams of extraterrestrials and robots slaying the human race.
10:43pm

 KingofSlack People can be so judgmental.
10:45pm

WiseOneWP There is no way I'm getting any sleep tonight.

11:15pm

 KingofSlack@WiseOneWP DUDE! Get online, we can do some serious RP gaming!

11:20pm

 WiseOneWP@KingofSlack I can't. I'm a mess. I think I just tried to break it off with Claire as JD. And failed.

11:21pm

 WiseOneWP@KingofSlack What is wrong with me?

11:22pm

 KingofSlack@WiseOneWP Not sure where to start. But you know what would help?

11:25pm

 WiseOneWP@KingofSlack Besides pulling a Miley and quitting Twitter? No, what?

11:30pm

 KingofSlack@WiseOneWP Get online and start playing! We can totally take the genius ten-year-old from Russia!

11:35pm

 WiseOneWP Why do I even try?

11:37pm

BIG MOUTH B

The Boy Who Cried Wolf . . . should have kept his mouth shut!

Friday, March 26, 9:09am

When we are little, our parents read us all these fairy tales and we blindly accept that they are good and moral and full of valuable life lessons. They aren't. Or, rather, I should say that the true lessons we are supposed to get from them are often missed. As a result, girls only learn that they need a prince charming who is heroic and dashing and a bit of a drama king. So they fail to see the good guy, who is somewhat not as charming in the looks department, standing there waiting to sweep her off her feet. Or at least open the door to his beat-up car and give her a ride to a party. And from these same stories, guys believe that they can pretty much do anything as long as they are charming about it and they will have the storybook ending to whatever chapter they are on.

As one of the not-so-charming prince charmings, I've become increasingly annoyed with the stories that are perpetuating the myths. And, after some rather disturbing news was brought to my attention, it occurred to me that the boy who cried wolf is the only story that has any sort of realistic ending. In this particular case, the boy is a friend of mine who has, instead of crying wolf, cried love . . . or at least attention. And in answer—a girl, who, like the villagers in the story who believed there was a wolf—believed this attention was real. Now, as the boy continues to cry wolf and the girl continues to believe it, they get into darker and darker territory. And what will happen in the end? Will the wolf—or love—become real and turn on the boy who screamed its name? Or, will the girl figure out the game soon enough to put a stop to it before too many people are hurt?

The point of this hard-to-follow post is simple. The boy needs to stop. Right now. 'Cause the villagers are getting restless and they are going to turn on him . . . it's as sure as Prince Charming riding in to save the day.

Lots0love #The Desperate Wannabes are playing! Woot-woot!

Friday, March 26, 4:44pm

 KingofSlack #The Desperate Wannabes. This is better than when Joss Whedon spoke at USC!

4:56pm

 WiseOneWP Dork! *RT@KingofSlack This is better than when Joss Whedon spoke at USC!*

4:59pm

 KingofSlack I'm determined to ignore my ignorant friends and enjoy the Wannabes. You know who you are, ignorant friends.

5:15pm

 KingofSlack@WiseOneWP Dork? You are the one who KEEPS tweeting!! Dude.

5:20pm

 KingofSlack@WiseOneWP Should I just start tweeting you @TopofGame17? Would that be better for you?

5:21pm

 WiseOneWP Oh so now my friend decides to act like a friend and not a brain-dead gamer geek and finally talk about real life. Nice.

5:21pm

KingofSlack@WiseOneWP Real? U want to talk about real? What happened to the "only one time" rule? Threw that one out the window apparently
5:30pm

 WiseOneWP@KingofSlack I know. I get it. I want it to be a logical end, that's all. Not just disappear.
5:31pm

 KingofSlack@WiseOneWP Dude, logical would have been stopping when we planned. Not going on and on.
5:34pm

 WiseOneWP@KingofSlack You are not entirely wrong. But I can't help it if she tweets me!
5:40pm

 ClaireRBear Timing couldn't be better. No horse show. Big Wannabes show coming up. I'm in!
5:56pm

 Lots0love This is going to be the concert to end all concerts!!
5:58pm

Lots0love For big night on the town, do I go full-on makeup or is it light and fresh?
9:10pm

 KingofSlack Just got home from driving brother around. Fun times. Fun times indeed.
9:11pm

 ClaireRBear@Lots0love We need a sleepover. Now. Can you borrow car from Emma? Or Harris?
9:13pm

 Lots0love@ClaireRBear Sure bear. What's up? I'll be over in twenty.
9:15pm

 ClaireRBear@Lots0love I have a JD update and tweets to show you. Need your help "interpreting."
9:15pm

 Lots0love@ClaireRBear Then it is your lucky day. I'm an expert interpreter. See you soon.
9:17pm

 ClaireRBear Yay! Girls night in before the girls night out!
9:20pm

KingofSlack@ClaireRBear Why you gotta be so separatist? It's no fun unless I'm there. *RT@ ClaireRBear Yay! Girls night in before the girls night out!*
9:20pm

 ClaireRBear@KingofSlack Ah, Benn. I will miss you but think we spend enough time together, don't you? Plus, if you came, all you'd do is fight with Lottie.
9:25pm

 KingofSlack@ClaireRBear Is it my fault that she is drawn to my rugged physique and acts like a crazy person whenever she sees me?
9:25pm

 ClaireRBear@KingofSlack Is that what it is? My bad. Thought she just hated your guts. I'll let her know.
9:25pm

 KingofSlack@ClaireRBear Sadly, I imagine u will. While u give each other back rubs during your panty tickle pillow fights. Can I drop my camera off?
9:26pm

 ClaireRBear@KingofSlack Gross! Benn! It's a good thing I have known you forever or else I'd have to agree with Lots that you are a giant pig.
9:26pm

 KingofSlack@ClaireRBear Maybe Will and I will dress up like ninjas and scare u.
9:26pm

 Lots0love On my way. Season one of Gossip Girl in my hand! Start popping the corn and bust out the sugary soda. We are going hog wild, I say.
9:36pm

Lots0love A fabulous night behind me. A fantastic one ahead of me. Woo-hoo!
Saturday, March 27, 1:12pm

 ClaireRBear Couldn't agree more. *RT@Lots0love A fabulous night behind me. A fantastic one ahead of me. Woo-hoo!*
1:15pm

 WiseOneWP@Lots0love Sorry about the interruption of girls night. I tried to talk Benn out of it but you know how he gets.
1:20pm

 Lots0love@WiseOneWP Do you mean I know how he is totally immature and annoying and I'm sure was just hoping to catch us in middle of pillow fight?
1:21pm

 WiseOneWP@Lots0love I think Benn would prefer to catch you in the middle of a Lord of Rings role-playing game.
1:22pm

 KingofSlack I take offense at being spoken of in such a cruel and heartless manner.
1:25pm

 Lots0love@WiseOneWP Look at you being witty, Mr. Parker. Always took you for the shy guy.
1:26pm

 WiseOneWP@Lots0love I'm full of surprises. Trust me.
1:30pm

Lots0love@WiseOneWP Sure you are.

1:31pm

 KingofSlack I must say, though, seeing y'all dressed up as orcs would be pretty darn hawt. Perhaps inspiration for Halloween next year?

1:45pm

 Lots0love You are ridiculous. *RT@KingofSlack I must say, though, seeing y'all dressed up as orcs would be pretty darn hawt.*

1:46pm

 Lots0love@ClaireRBear I'm still so impressed with the JD thing. He thinks you are great!!

1:51pm

 ClaireRBear@Lots0love IDK. What is with the "I'm not into Twitter" thing. If he would just talk to me in person I'd understand.

1:53pm

 Lots0love@ClaireRBear Give it a little time Bear. Go listen to all your Wannabes songs to prepare for concert! Who knows, he could be there!

2:05pm

 ClaireRBear@Lots0love I might just ask him about that. Like you said last night, just cause he doesn't like Twitter doesn't mean I can't try to talk to him.

2:07pm

Lots0love@ClaireRBear That's my girl! Be bold!
2:07pm

 ClaireRBear@Lots0love Here I go. Wish me luck.
2:08pm

 Lots0love Thank God for teacher training days. Concert on Sunday is not a problem when parents don't have reason to keep you home!
2:10pm

ClaireRBear@TopofGame17 Hey, any chance you're heading to Wannabes tomorrow?
2:08pm

 ClaireRBear I keep hearing the theme song from Jeopardy playing over and over in my head. I'll take Mysteries for $1000, Alex.
3:00pm

 TopofGame17@ClaireRBear Hey there. So was girls night everything u hoped? Did u talk about me?
3:07pm

 ClaireRBear@TopofGame17 You read that, huh?
3:13pm

 TopofGame17@ClaireRBear I said I'm not good at talking on this thing, not that I don't follow!
3:15pm

 ClaireRBear@TopofGame17 Ah, I see, the stalker approach.
3:16pm

 ClaireRBear@TopofGame17 PS—way to avoid concert question! You should think about being a lawyer when you get done with school.
3:52pm

 TopofGame17@ClaireRBear Think I'll stick with journalism but thanks for the career advice
3:55pm

ClaireRBear@TopofGame17 Journalism? Never would have called that. Would think writer would like tweeting. Which you don't, remember?
3:57pm

 ClaireRBear@TopofGame17 Hey, why don't you work for the school paper?
4:00pm

 Lots0love Off to Chick. Send orders to my cell if you are hungry!
4:02pm

 KingofSlack@Lots0love Waffle Fries! *RT@Lots0love Off to Chick. Send orders to my cell if you are hungry!*
4:05pm

 Lots0love@KingofSlack I meant Claire you moron. Why would I ever buy you anything?
4:10pm

 KingofSlack@Lots0love Someday u will realize you love me.
4:11pm

 Lots0love@KingofSlack Tcha. When hell freezes over.
4:20pm

TopofGame17@ClaireRBear Oh. Well, tweeting and writing articles are different. Paper conflicted with sports I guess. Going to follow through in college
4:20pm

 ClaireRBear@TopofGame17 Cool! If you ever need advice, you know where to reach me.
4:21pm

 TopofGame17@ClaireRBear I certainly do. For someone clueless, you give great advice.
4:22pm

 Lots0love The countdown can truly and officially begin. Only a day away from musical bliss.
5:03pm

 ClaireRBear Must get head out of clouds. Wish I knew how to compartmentalize! Chix nuggets please, Lots!!
6:24pm

 ClaireRBear@TopofGame17 Sorry. Me again. Know you don't like tweeting, but realized you still never answered concert question
8:00pm

 TopofGame17@ClaireRBear Would be fun. Love their song "Overlapping."
8:10pm

ClaireRBear@TopofGame17 That's my favorite song!! I always change the line where they say, "sweet dreams sweet Blair" to "sweet dreams sweet Claire."

8:10pm

 ClaireRBear@TopofGame17 So you aren't going to concert?

8:36pm

 TopofGame17@ClaireRBear Sadly no. I have lax tournament. But have a good time.

8:40pm

 ClaireRBear@TopofGame17 Too bad! I'm sure you'll hear all about it. Have a good night!

8:41pm

 TopofGame17@ClaireRBear You too. Night Tweets.

9:13pm

 ClaireRBear@TopofGame17 Tweets?

9:14pm

 TopofGame17@ClaireRBear Yup. Short for Ms. Tweetso'Lot. Get it?

9:14pm

 ClaireRBear@TopofGame17 Ah, got it. Well, night Mr. Whitcomb. Till next time I bother you . . .

9:15pm

BIG MOUTH B

To go or not to go . . .
or more specifically, to go out or stay in
and watch Battlestar.

Saturday, March 27, 10:43am

Hello boys and girls. It is I, your wise and caring
Uncle Big Mouth. Another weekend is upon us
and I'm sure many of you are still lying under your
covers recovering from post-Friday night coma. I
have sacrificed my own sleep to impart a few
more wise words. Be grateful, dear readers. My
scandalous Friday night consisted of a rousing
game of Resident Evil with my little brother followed
by milk and cake and driving said brother to his
buddy's so that *they* could go out. You should
never drink and drive, but what can I say? I'm a
born rebel. Lucky the cops were busy busting the
party over at Ryan K.'s house.

So while you recover from your fun and I recover
from my humiliation of another night of lameness, I
figured it would be good to go over some rules
about—you guessed it—socializing. We all know
there is the required hierarchy at every school. It
varies depending on school to a degree (I mean,
doubtful that at a performing arts school the

basketball players would be the kings of the court, so to speak—unless you go to that school in High School Musical. That just threw the whole equation off. Usually, there are those who rule, those who follow, and those who just say screw it (i.e. the losers and outcasts). We stick to our own kind in some sort of weird high school evolution of the fittest.

My kind is the, shall we say, less social kind. We find comfort in routine and in the warmth of our own living rooms. Or at least we tell ourselves we do. Some of us just aren't invited to anything. I like to think I choose.

On this Saturday, I am once again faced with the question—to go out or not to go out? Out is where the "others" are—the cool people with their perfect clothes and hair. You know the ones. The Deltas and Craigs of the South who have been bred to look perfect. However, Out is also where the fun is. Tomorrow night's fun is in the form of a killer concert. Now, I love the band. I love the music. I love the venue. But do I love feeling like an outsider? Not so much. I have a couple friends to go with, and there is strength in numbers, so I might be saved some humiliation. But no guarantee . . . so do I dare?

And I think . . . the answer is yes. True, I'm not a lacrosse player, but in my world, I rule. Because what the popular crowd fails to recognize is that the geeks have hierarchies too. Geeks over nerds, Battlestarlets over Trekkies, biology brains over calc cutthroats. It is a dog-eat-dork world my friends and I am a dog who can eat a few dorks. Or at least I've never been eaten by a dog. Or something.

What I'm trying to say is, tomorrow I will go. I will dance. I will most probably make a fool of myself. But by the fluff of my over-worn and extremely manly fuzzy slippers, I can't spend another night on the couch while my younger brother goes out and parties. I just ask that if you see me in the corner, please ignore me like you usually do . . . I'll do the same.

WiseOneWP@KingofSlack So Big Mouth, where do I fall in the dork-archy??
Sunday, March 28, 4:12pm

 KingofSlack@WiseOneWP You have such potential to be part of the cool crowd. But you shun them.
4:20pm

 KingofSlack@WiseOneWP Embrace your good looks and use your brain for good, and sometimes wily, purposes.
4:21pm

 KingofSlack@WiseOneWP Plus, you like Syfy channel enough to still call it by its old-school name— SciFi . In my book, you are at the top of the dork-archy
4:21pm

 KingofSlack@WiseOneWP Well, not exactly top but pretty close. I'm at the very top.
4:22pm

 WiseOneWP@KingofSlack LOL. Of course you are. I'm but a humble minion.
4:30pm

 KingofSlack@WiseOneWP You are truly wise. Though sometimes I think it might be nice to roll with JD and his crew.
4:31pm

 KingofSlack@WiseOneWP Oh, wait! I DO. I hang with you. HAAAA!
4:32pm

WiseOneWP@KingofSlack Very funny. Seriously, just busted a gut. Have you thought about stand up?
4:37pm

 KingofSlack@WiseOneWP I don't think it would be fair to other comedians.
4:40pm

 WiseOneWP@KingofSlack You know I feel terrible.
4:40pm

 KingofSlack@WiseOneWP Here's an idea. Why don't u just come clean? U had great opportunity at your house the other night.
4:41pm

 WiseOneWP@KingofSlack If, hypothetically, I were to tell her the truth, do you know what would happen?
4:42pm

 KingofSlack@WiseOneWP This farce would end and we could get on with our lives?
4:43pm

 WiseOneWP@KingofSlack OR she would a) kill me and b) never talk to me again. So I'd be dead AND have zero chance of her liking me.
4:45pm

 WiseOneWP@KingofSlack I can't tell her the truth. It just needs to fade. Which it will. It has to.
4:47pm

 KingofSlack@WiseOneWP Did it ever occur to u that she would have talked to u before if u had tried?
4:48pm

KingofSlack@WiseOneWP U got yourself into this, u can get yourself out. Now, I'm going to catch us a ride with B and Lottie to the concert. U in?
4:48pm

 WiseOneWP@KingofSlack In like Flynn
4:50pm

 KingofSlack@WiseOneWP Tron Baby!! Nice one. G2G!
4:55pm

 WiseOneWP@KingofSlack Listen, I am going to stop. Really. She tweeted JD and "he" told her he wasn't going to the concert.
5:01pm

 WiseOneWP@KingofSlack That is the end of it . . .
5:01pm

 KingofSlack@WiseOneWP Whatever u say. Let's hope real JD isn't going!
5:03pm

 WiseOneWP@KingofSlack Guys lax team has tournament. He should be AWOL
5:05pm

 KingofSlack@WiseOneWP Look at you, getting all sly. Should I be proud? Or worried?
5:07pm

KingofSlack Check out **#Wannabesrock!**
5:30pm

 KingofSlack Also don't forget to check out Big Mouth B! Wisdom at the touch of a key. Or at least procrastination at the touch of a key.
5:31pm

 Lots0love Wannabes + my boyfriend + my best friend = priceless!
6:30pm

 Lots0love + two tagalongs = ugh!
6:31pm

ClaireRBear My purse is packed and I'm ready to go. Where oh where is my ride?

8:02pm

 Lots0love@ClaireRBear I'm on my way silly girl. Had to put on my face as they say down here. Y'all dolled up? You talked to you know who again?

8:08pm

 ClaireRBear@Lots0love I think you should get your butt over here so we can discuss in person. Move it L! Time's a tickin.

8:08pm

 Lots0love@ClaireRBear On my way. Ford will honk when we get there.

8:10pm

 ClaireRBear Argh!!! WHERE IS MY RIDE???

8:30pm

 WiseOneWP@ClaireRBear@KingofSlack Really OK if Benn and I come with? Not butting in on anything?

8:31pm

 ClaireRBear@WiseOneWP OMG! No! I wouldn't want to see the Wannabes with anybody else!

8:32pm

 ClaireRBear@WiseOneWP Well, not entirely true. But JD said he wasn't going. Did I tell you I tweeted him??

8:33pm

ClaireRBear@WiseOneWP Lottie and I talked about it. Definitely some serious flirting. Can you believe it???

8:34pm

 WiseOneWP@ClaireRBear You talked to Lottie about it? Yeah, wow.

8:34pm

 ClaireRBear@WiseOneWP I know! But don't worry, you and Benn are still my boys.

8:35pm

 WiseOneWP@ClaireRBear Fantastic

8:35pm

 KingofSlack We are going to bring the desperate to the Wannabes. Watch out dance floor.

8:36pm

 ClaireRBear Note to self: Learn to keep your head and heart in check you crazy girl. AND watch out for Benn's crazy desperate feet.

8:37pm

BIG MOUTH B

Too exhausted to type . . . but Wannabes ROCKED!

Monday, March 29, 1:43am

More to come tomorrow. Promise. Or maybe day after. It really depends on when I get feeling back in my fingers. And toes. Not that I can type with my toes but would just like to have sensation in them again. I knew I shouldn't have stood so close to the flailing masses. Have to recover, but it is safe to say . . . I'm glad I chose GO!

Lots0love I heart you Desperate Wannabes. You touch my soul and make me want to fly.

Monday, March 29, 11:23am

 Lots0love Best concert ever!!! Three sets! Two encores! When they sang "everytime you speak, the heart beats, beats, beats," my heart beat beat beat

11:23am

 Lots0love Once again, thank you teachers of Watkins Prep for giving us the day off.

11:24am

 ClaireRBear@Lots0love Think your heart beat due more to Ford than lyrics.

11:30am

 Lots0love@ClaireRBear IDK . . . not so much really. Did you see the way he danced?? Looked like he had full body tic going.

11:30am

 ClaireRBear@Lots0love He was NOT that bad.

11:33am

 KingofSlack What was that? I can't hear you. Deaf from concert. SO worth it.

11:33am

KingofSlack@Lots0love Yo. Your boy's got some smooth moves.
11:35am

 Lots0love@KingofSlack Whatever. He was just doing an imitation of you.
11:37am

 KingofSlack@Lots0love Hey, if that helps u sleep at night . . .
11:40am

 Lots0love@ClaireRBear Crap. Even Jones is making fun of him. This is bad. So so bad.
11:41am

 ClaireRBear@Lots0love You are NOT going to break up with him just b/c he can't dance. Are you?
11:42am

 Lots0love@ClaireRBear He's not the perfect prince. You should understand my pain.
11:45am

 ClaireRBear@Lots0love After last night, I'm not sure what to think about princes. They are more confusing than ever.
11:46am

 ClaireRBear@Lots0love Much prefer to read about fictional love. Like Elizabeth and Darcy.
11:46am

ClaireRBear@Lots0love Or Romeo and Juliet

11:47am

 ClaireRBear@Lots0love Edward and Bella

11:47am

 Lots0love@ClaireRBear Or perhaps like Lottie and Johnny L.

11:48am

 ClaireRBear@Lots0love Is that Ford's replacement? Like it—love story of 16 yr old girl from SC and the lead singer of a famous band.

11:50am

 Lots0love@ClaireRBear That has best seller written all over it. Or maybe more Lifetime special . . .

11:51am

 ClaireRBear@Lots0love Don't mean to be selfish, but can we PLEASE focus on the JD run-in??

11:58am

 Lots0love@ClaireRBear My bad. What happened? It can't have been THAT bad, right?

12:01pm

 Lots0love@ClaireRBear I mean, you didn't walk up and say "Is there an airport nearby cuz I think my heart just took off."

12:03pm

ClaireRBear@Lots0love LOL! But seriously L, I have no idea what's going on. He acted like he hardly knew who I was.

12:05pm

 ClaireRBear@Lots0love And of course Will and Bennett saw whole thing!

12:05pm

 Lots0love@ClaireRBear I'm sorry. I should have been there. Was trying to protect world from Ford's flying arms. What happened exactly?

12:06pm

 KingofSlack More news at **#wannabesrock**. Coverage of the show and set list! Must check it out.

12:06pm

 KingofSlack No news of my appearance at **#wannabesrock**. I must remedy.

12:06pm

 Lots0love@ClaireRBear Why is Benn so weird? I mean does he honestly think anyone cared he was there??

12:07pm

ClaireRBear@Lots0love Focus! Again, it was so bizarre. First of all, JD wasn't even supposed to be at the concert. He TOLD me he wasn't going!

12:07pm

ClaireRBear@Lots0love And I wore that ridiculous tight shirt you said made me look curvalicious but am pretty sure just makes me look fat!

12:08pm

 Lots0love@ClaireRBear It did not!

12:09pm

 ClaireRBear@Lots0love Whatevs, not the point. You & Ford were all over each other so Will, Benn and I went down front to get closer to the band. JD was there.

12:10pm

 Lots0love@ClaireRBear Teach you to ever go anywhere with those two . . . I kid. Actually kind of had fun with them last night . . .

12:11pm

 KingofSlack Still can't hear you. And gosh darnit, have serious television to watch!!

12:20pm

 KingofSlack I guess temporary deafness is a small price to pay.

12:21pm

 ClaireRBear@Lots0love Glad to hear the boys didn't cramp your style, but as I was SAYING . . .

12:28pm

ClaireRBear@Lots0love So I walked up and said hey, I thought you weren't coming tonight.
12:30pm

 ClaireRBear@Lots0love Because, I repeat, THAT WAS WHAT HE TOLD ME.
12:30pm

 ClaireRBear@Lots0love And . . . he just said, "excuse me?"
12:31pm

 ClaireRBear@Lots0love I sort of stood there for a sec with my mouth hanging open. Real attractive huh?
12:32pm

 ClaireRBear@Lots0love And then I just blurted out something about lax game and finally he laughed and said yeah, he couldn't miss the concert.
12:33pm

 ClaireRBear@Lots0love THEN he asked me if I liked Wannabes which is weird b/c he knows I do. I don't know. It was so AWK!
12:33pm

 ClaireRBear@Lots0love Then he sort of shrugged and said bye and walked away.
12:34pm

 ClaireRBear@Lots0love I don't get it. This is what I get for trying to flirt.
12:35pm

 Lots0love@ClaireRBear OK, wow. Well, he DID talk to you so maybe he was just playing it cool . . .
12:36pm

ClaireRBear@Lots0love But you've seen the tweets! He flirts with me!! I don't get it. I'm such a freak!!!
12:37pm

 Lots0love@ClaireRBear You are not! There has to be a logical explanation. We'll get to bottom of it. Promise.
12:40pm

 ClaireRBear Don't have much faith in logical explanations.
12:41pm

 Lots0love Emma wants to hear all about the concert. Ugh. I can't stand caring parents.
12:45pm

KingofSlack Going to school after long weekend is always doubly worse. Add amazing concert to mix and it's all over.
5:03pm

 WiseOneWP Agreed. Tuesday is going to feel like Monday. *RT@KingofSlack Going to school after long weekend is always doubly worse.*
5:34pm

 LotsOlove Another boy bites the dust.
6:13pm

 LotsOlove@ClaireRBear Hey little bear, u still blue?
6:15pm

 ClaireRBear@LotsOlove I forgot about it for about an hour while at barn. All came rushing back. I can't show my face tmrw
6:30pm

 ClaireRBear@LotsOlove Wait? Did you break up with Ford???
6:30pm

 ClaireRBear Check out great reviews of concert! http:tiny.cc/GyGa5
6:34pm

Lots0love@ClaireRBear Yeah, that is over. Wasn't going to go anywhere anyway.
6:40pm

 ClaireRBear@Lots0love Sorry to hear that. You okay?
6:41pm

 Lots0love@ClaireRBear Never better. Enough about me. I'm worried bout you. YOU okay?
6:44pm

 ClaireRBear@Lots0love Sure, if I never ever see JD again. Ever.
6:46pm

 ClaireRBear@Lots0love Seriously, what do I do if I see him tmrw?? Do I act like nothing happened?
6:47pm

 Lots0love@ClaireRBear That's what I would do. Just lay low . . . wait for him to come to you
6:48pm

 ClaireRBear@Lots0love Don't know if I can manage that. No good at acting. I'll probably blurt something the second I see him.
6:50pm

 WiseOneWP@KingofSlack@ClaireRBear Hey y'all. Need to start planning the senior edition of paper this wk.
6:52pm

KingofSlack@ClaireRBear@WiseOneWP Listen, overachiever, we'll get to it in time. Yo Claire, recover from the run-in?

6:53pm

 ClaireRBear@KingofSlack@WiseOneWP You are a laugh riot Benn. And FYI, I'm thinking of moving to Alaska. Or joining a nunnery. Maybe both.

6:53pm

 KingofSlack@ClaireRBear@WiseOneWP We'll miss you. The same way we miss gym class.

6:54pm

 ClaireRBear@KingofSlack@WiseOneWP Knock it off. Do you want me to tell your readers you still sleep with your "bankie"? Oh. oops.

7:00pm

 WiseOneWP@ClaireRBear@KingofSlack Children, behave. Claire—don't move to Alaska. Need your help on paper. And we'd really miss you. Benn, play nice.

7:01pm

 KingofSlack@WiseOneWP@ClaireRBear Oh that's just priceless coming from you. Mr. Sensitive and Sincere himself.

7:02pm

 ClaireRBear@KingofSlack@WiseOneWP What are you talking about? Benn—why are you being so mean?

7:05pm

 KingofSlack I'm out. I don't need this.

7:15pm

From: **ParkerWill.2010@gmail.com**
Sent: Monday, March 29, 10:24pm
To: BennettJonesEsq@gmail.com
Subject: Help a man out

Okay, I messed up. You are right to be pissed. I shouldn't have told Claire that JD wasn't going to concert. I NEVER thought he would actually be there! He was supposed to be at a freaking lacrosse tournament, like 200 miles away. Who has the energy to go to a concert after playing all day? What is he? Freaking Superman?

You heard Claire talking to him, right? I mean we were standing right there. What if he starts talking back now? How long is it going to take before she asks him about something "he" tweeted? And then how long until he draws a blank? This is JD. It will take all of two seconds. And as soon as she realizes he was never on Twitter, she's going to figure this all out. And you know what happens then? I'm dead to her.

Any more brilliant ideas in that head of yours? Or are you going to leave me alone to stew in my own pot of burning hot angst? Probably. Because I brought this on myself. Oh wait. Not entirely. It was YOUR genius idea that got this started in the first place. So how about helping a man out? Please??

—Will

From: **BennettJonesEsq@gmail.com**
Sent: Monday, March 29, 11:43PM
To: ParkerWill.2010@gmail.com
Subject: Told you so

Dear idiot,

I take offense at the tone of your email and the accusations you throw my way. I dared offer up the plan to help my boy out. You were the one who took it beyond. As previously stated and suggested, my advice—or brilliant backup plan if you will—is quite revolutionary. Tell her the truth. I think she can handle it. Sometimes honesty really is the best policy. Far better for you to do it now than for her to figure it out when JD, as you fear, does talk to her.

Benn

From: **ParkerWill.2010@gmail.com**
Sent: Tuesday, March 30, 12:02am
To: BennettJonesEsq@gmail.com
Subject: Re: Told you so

Thanks, Einstein.

Of course I'm not going to tell her the truth. How many times do I have to tell you that if I do that, she'll never speak to me again? At this point, I'm just doing damage control and praying for a miracle. Which would consist of JD never talking to Claire, her getting over JD and moving on, and all suspicion evaporating. What are the odds? Don't tell me. Not good.

But I can't tell her! I just can't. Where would I even start?

Off to eat hot coals and poke eyeballs with sticks,
Will

Lots0love Time to start searching again . . .
Tuesday, March 30, 8:56am

KingofSlack Time to start getting more sleep. This beautiful physique needs royal treatment.
8:56am

ClaireRBear@Lots0love You know what? Screw playing it cool. I'm going to call JD out on it.
9:04am

Lots0love@ClaireRBear You go girl. Take deep breaths. Remember, he doesn't know how embarrassed you are.
9:05am

Lots0love Ew boy. I think there might be a fireworks show y'all.
9:06am

KingofSlack Fireworks? I like fireworks. *RT@Lots0love Ew boy. I think there might be a fireworks show y'all.*
9:10am

WiseOneWP Fireworks are only good at Fourth of July. *RT@KingofSlack Fireworks? I like fireworks.*
9:15am

ClaireRBear@TopofGame17 Question: what was with you last night?
9:15am

 ClaireRBear@Lots0love He hasn't responded. I'm getting the picture.
12:26pm

 Lots0love@ClaireRBear Deep breaths. He has probably been in class this whole time. Just wait.
12:30pm

 Lots0love Sending out happy thoughts. Don't give up!
12:32pm

 Lots0love Why does everything have to be such a game?
12:35pm

 TopofGame17@ClaireRBear Hey. Yeah, sorry bout being all weird at the concert. You know how it is.
12:37pm

 ClaireRBear@TopofGame17 Actually, I don't really know how it is. You talk to me on Twitter, say we're friends, and then in person, you totally blow me off.
12:40pm

ClaireRBear@TopofGame17 You said you weren't even going.
12:40pm

 ClaireRBear@TopofGame17 And, I mean, why would you pretend like you didn't know if I liked the Wannabes?
12:41pm

 TopofGame17@ClaireRBear IDK. I guess I was all thrown off my game. I get nervous sometimes.
12:45pm

 TopofGame17@ClaireRBear I really am sorry. For what it's worth.
12:48pm

 TopofGame17@ClaireRBear It wasn't my intention to upset you. Or lie. I hate lying.
12:50pm

 ClaireRBear@TopofGame17 Huh. Ok. Apology sort of accepted, Mr. Whitcomb. I know all about getting nervous. I just didn't think you did that.
12:51pm

 TopofGame17@ClaireRBear Well yeah. I'm human.
12:52pm

 ClaireRBear@TopofGame17 Me too. See you around. Don't be a stranger. Maybe say hi?
12:53pm

TopofGame17@ClaireRBear Yeah, ok. Maybe!
12:54pm

ClaireRBear I'm really beginning to enjoy spring. Time for some column action. Anybody got a question? Send my way. Get Clueless!
1:00pm

KingofSlack The first Spring Fling poster is up in the hallways. Let the girly screeching begin.
1:05pm

Lots0love New search has new criteria. Need to find someone with dancing moves. I'm NOT going to spring fling with flying arms.
1:15pm

From: **ClaireBearR16@gmail.com**
Sent: Tuesday, March 30, 1:20pm
To: LottieM17@gmail.com
Subject: Update?

Okay, so call me crazy (or maybe a bit desperate), but I think, despite his weird behavior at the concert, that JD is not such a bad guy. Believe it or not, Jack Dyson Whitcomb admitted that he got nervous when he tried to talk to me in person. So there, Jessica "I'm too cool cause my boobs are big" Mayers!

Can you believe it? I mean, this is JD! As in one of the hottest guys in the senior class. As in the guy in my Spanish class sophomore year that I could never talk to because every time I opened my mouth to TRY to speak to him, nothing but squeaks came out. (Okay, I didn't actually squeak but I might as well have, while a chorus of crickets echoed in the background.) The guy who has led WP to three straight state titles in lacrosse. The guy who turned down a scholarship to UCLA to be closer to his sick mom. (Or so I've heard.) THAT GUY. He gets nervous! Around me!!!

I think I might be going into shock. If I don't show

up at school tomorrow, please send someone to see if I'm dead. It could happen. My heart is literally beating so hard I feel like it might break a rib or two (is that possible? IDK. I'll have to look up).

xoxo
Bear

KingofSlack Fully recovered from weekend debauchery. What's that? Oh yes, I can hear you again my friends.
1:21pm

 Lots0love@KingofSlack Friends plural! Congrats Benn, didn't know you had more than one.
1:22pm

 KingofSlack@Lots0love I'm busting a gut over here Matthews. You are like the wittiest girl at WP
1:23pm

 Lots0love@KingofSlack Don't I know it. So who do you have to talk to now that Claire is moving on?
1:25pm

 KingofSlack@Lots0love Go bother someone else. I have work to do.
1:30pm

 KingofSlack Time to post people. Need to supply the masses with their doses of lessons and gossip
1:32pm

 ClaireRBear Need something more fulfilling than gossip? Check out my top ten horse books. http://tiny.cc/GyGa5
1:35pm

 KingofSlack@WiseOneWP Dude. Re: your email from yesterday—you might be right to be freaking out.
1:42pm

WiseOneWP@KingofSlack ????

1:43pm

 KingofSlack@WiseOneWP JD came up to me at lunch and asked me about "that little horse chick."

1:45pm

 KingofSlack@WiseOneWP I smelled interest. And really bad cologne. Dude must bathe in that stuff.

1:45pm

 WiseOneWP@KingofSlack You're joking right? This is like a really funny way to get me back for not listening to you, right?

1:48pm

 KingofSlack@WiseOneWP Even I'm not that cruel. He said he'd seen her hanging around u and me. Asked if she was single—he actually said "hooked up"

1:50pm

 WiseOneWP@KingofSlack Make it stop

1:51pm

 KingofSlack@WiseOneWP No such luck. He's got his eye on her. His words. He said that in this pervy way.

1:53pm

 KingofSlack@WiseOneWP He's going to ask her out. Sorry dude. Looks like you are in for a world of hurt.

2:01pm

 WiseOneWP@KingofSlack Did he say anything else? Like what he meant by his "eye on her"? If he does anything to hurt her . . .

2:03pm

KingofSlack@WiseOneWP Don't know what to tell you. He asked a few questions. I may have mentioned she writes Get Clueless.

2:05pm

 KingofSlack@WiseOneWP Maybe it's not so bad. He really might like her. U do, so not entirely unbelievable others would. Although, he is a playa . . .

2:07pm

 WiseOneWP@KingofSlack You are not helping. This is ALL sorts of wrong. What if they go out?? Stuff I tweeted is bound to come up.

2:07pm

 KingofSlack@WiseOneWP Like I said—you made the bed, or I guess in this case you made the pile of crap.

2:08pm

 WiseOneWP@KingofSlack Thanks Benn. Your sympathy is really touching. I'm going to go throw up now. Then I'm going to figure out what to do.

2:10pm

 WiseOneWP@KingofSlack No, I already know what to do. Nothing. I can't do anything at all. Can I?

2:11pm

 KingofSlack@WiseOneWP Guess not. Unless maybe . . . Nah, forget it.

2:12pm

 WiseOneWP@KingofSlack WHAT???

2:15pm

KingofSlack@WiseOneWP It's a long shot, but . . .
2:17pm

 WiseOneWP@KingofSlack I swear man, just freaking spill. I know you are in study hall. I can come find you.
2:18pm

 KingofSlack@WiseOneWP Jeez. Grumpy much? There's SOME chance if u told JD the truth, he'd keep your cover.
2:20pm

 KingofSlack@WiseOneWP After all, u kind of did him a favor. You know, in a sick, unintentional way. By hooking him up with Claire.
2:21pm

 KingofSlack@WiseOneWP Sorry, but u gotta admit it's kind of funny. I mean, bad b/c CC is my friend and all, but sort of funny.
2:22pm

 WiseOneWP@KingofSlack Downright hilarious. I can't stand the guy and I couldn't have set him up better.
2:23pm

 KingofSlack@WiseOneWP So u r going to talk to him?
2:23pm

 WiseOneWP@KingofSlack It's my only hope.
2:25pm

Tuesday, March 30, 2010

SOMETHING I DO KNOW . . .

It's been one wild week. And from the looks of my in-box, I'm not alone. I used to hate when people used the expression "when it rains, it pours." But I'm beginning to see its truth.

My apologies if I can't get to all your questions. I'm trying, but being Clueless, I have to occasionally reach out for help on these. It takes time! I'm working my way through. So enjoy this week's selection. And who knows, maybe when you read the answers, you'll be glad I didn't get to yours.

Dear Clueless,
I've had a crush on this girl forever. I finally asked her out and she said yes. What if she isn't everything I thought she was? Should I still date her?

—Worried About Ms. Right

Dear Worried,
First, congratulations. I've been in the same

boat. Well, not exactly the same. I'm a girl and you're a boy. But still, the fundamentals are the same, I think. If I had a crush on someone and asked them out, and there was a reason I liked them in the first place, that reason would still be there. Crushes are crushes because there is something there. So if she isn't exactly what you thought, don't give up right away. Perhaps she is as nervous as you are. And maybe, in time, she will reveal herself to be exactly what you imagined.

Dear Clueless,
My best friend in the world finally seems to have the chance to hook up with the boy of her dreams but I think she is holding herself back. How do I tell her to take the leap? It could be a fun fall!

—Love to Share

Dear Love,

Aren't you just the sweetest friend ever. I'm sure, if this person is truly your best friend in the entire world, she knows that you want her to try and leap. But it can be hard. Trust me. There is a lot of comfort in the known. It sounds like maybe this friend's situation is more unknown. Give her time. Let her figure it out. Most importantly, be there for her on the other side of the jump. You say it could be fun; for those of us who don't leap often, it sounds like it might hurt.

ClaireRBear Just found out why mom is always on computer—she is IMing. With guys! Ugh.

5:30pm

 KingofSlack Could be worse. Little brother just beat my high score. *RT@ClaireRBear Just found out why my mom is always on computer*

5:31pm

 Lots0love Mystery solved. She getting hot dates? *RT@ClaireRBear Just found out why my mom is always on computer*

5:32pm

 ClaireRBear@Lots0love So why did you write in to Clueless? You know I want to leap. Well, I mean now I know.

5:45pm

 Lots0love@ClaireRBear See? I just wanted you to write it out. Now's time for action! So?

5:50pm

 ClaireRBear@Lots0love So what?

5:51pm

 Lots0love@ClaireRBear DID HE TALK TO YOU TODAY?? Don't play coy with me

5:51pm

 ClaireRBear@Lots0love Not yet . . . but didn't see him. I'll keep you updated, promise.

5:53pm

Lots0love@ClaireRBear Ready for Spring Fling. Sort of. Is one-sleeve still in? Or we back to straps?
5:55pm

 ClaireRBear@Lots0love If you hadn't dumped Ford b/c he didn't dance like Jay Sean maybe you'd have a date for school's big dance
5:56pm

 Lots0love@ClaireRBear Sigh . . . luckily I think maybe John Walker is interested. We were talking after lax practice for like an hour
6:00pm

 ClaireRBear@Lots0love John Walker? Nice! He is a cutie—and friends with JD. Once again my plan for double dating can take effect. Get to work!
6:01pm

 ClaireRBear@Lots0love Who am I kidding? You don't have to work at it, you are naturally blessed with the flirtation gene.
6:03pm

 ClaireRBear@Lots0love You think there is a chance JD will ask me to Fling? I can't go with Benn AGAIN this yr.
7:10pm

 Lots0love@ClaireRBear Benn=No! JD=Yes! I have fingers and toes crossed for ya. Night darling.
9:41 pm

KingofSlack Am not going to sleep until I once again control the high score.
10:35pm

 KingofSlack Still not in control. Any one out there have **#rulestobeatvictoriousvillain**?
11:39pm

 KingofSlack Defeated.
Wednesday March 31, 1:05am

WiseOneWP@ClaireRBear Hey there. How's it going? You're missing the paper's lunch meeting.
12:06pm

 ClaireRBear@WiseOneWP Have to get an assignment done for lab. In library now. Take notes please? And OMG big news. Will tell you later. Have to talk to Lottie.
12:07pm

 WiseOneWP@ClaireRBear Um, okay. Sounds intriguing. I'll cover for you at meeting.
12:09pm

 ClaireRBear@Lots0love HE TALKED TO ME!!! In the student center! Eeks!!
12:12pm

 Lots0love@ClaireRBear HE DID??? What did he say?? What did he do? Deets, please!
12:13pm

 ClaireRBear@Lots0love I was just grabbing stuff out of my bag that I needed to bring home.
12:15pm

 ClaireRBear@Lots0love And he walked into StuCe with Blake Johnson. I told myself he'd walk right past me like always. But then he stopped
12:16pm

 ClaireRBear@Lots0love and said, "Hey Claire." Just like that. As though it were the most natural thing in the world for him to do.
12:16pm

Lots0love@ClaireRBear Nice. And then what?

12:21pm

 ClaireRBear@Lots0love What? Hey isn't enough for you?

12:21pm

 Lots0love@ClaireRBear Come on! Give a girl a break! Tell me he said something else . . .

12:22pm

 ClaireRBear@Lots0love Well, since you asked. After I squeaked hi back he said, "Sorry I didn't say hi sooner."

12:24pm

 ClaireRBear@Lots0love And then, wait for it, this is the best part . . .

12:26pm

 ClaireRBear@Lots0love He went to touch my shoulder and I jerked back cause I'm smooth like that

12:26pm

 ClaireRBear@Lots0love and he just laughed all sweet, then tugged my ponytail and said "talk to ya later." Sigh. I'm drooling a little.

12:27pm

 Lots0love@ClaireRBear Oh Bear!! I'm so happy for you! See—it's all about positive thinking.

12:30pm

ClaireRBear@Lots0love That MUST be it. Want to live it over and over in my mind.
12:30pm

 Lots0love@ClaireRBear Well, maybe he'll tweet you later and you can have that to look forward to.
12:31pm

 ClaireRBear@Lots0love This is why you are my best friend. Always keeping my chin up. Have fun at the game this afternoon!
12:59pm

KingofSlack@WiseOneWP Heads up. JD was flirting again with Claire today in StuCe.

3:05pm

 WiseOneWP@KingofSlack Thanks for the update. I figured something must have happened. Claire was all atwitter—pun intended.

3:06pm

 WiseOneWP@KingofSlack Can't wait for them to talk more.

3:11pm

 KingofSlack@WiseOneWP Sarcasm is not becoming on u my friend. Have u talked to him yet?

3:15pm

 WiseOneWP@KingofSlack Um, sort of. I mean I tried to explain the sitch but I think it might have gone over his head.

3:16pm

 KingofSlack@WiseOneWP Does that surprise you? Did you use small words? That helps.

3:18pm

 WiseOneWP@KingofSlack Can anything really help at this point?

3:18pm

 KingofSlack@WiseOneWP Enough with the whining already. You're worse than LC in season two of The Hills.

3:18pm

 WiseOneWP@KingofSlack My apologies that life is a mess and am upset.

3:19pm

KingofSlack@WiseOneWP Back to the story?
3:19pm

 WiseOneWP@KingofSlack I just told JD that I had tweeted with CC a few times and she had thought she was talking to him. Too complicated to explain rest.
3:19pm

 WiseOneWP@KingofSlack And then I told him not to say anything and roll with it if she mentioned something "he" had said.
3:21pm

 KingofSlack@WiseOneWP That's good right? What u wanted?
3:25pm

 WiseOneWP@KingofSlack Exactly what I wanted. I even wanted him to then say "thanks dude for the hookup." Perfect.
3:26pm

 WiseOneWP@KingofSlack Anyway, now I just have to hope he sticks to his end of deal which I think he will cause it's easy enough for him.
3:33pm

 KingofSlack@WiseOneWP Crisis averted. All is good.
3:36pm

 WiseOneWP@KingofSlack Yup. All good. Freaking perfect.
3:36pm

KingofSlack@WiseOneWP U said it, not me.
3:37pm

 KingofSlack Me and my trekkies are going to get beam on at a convention!
3:42pm

 ClaireRBear@KingofSlack You are such a geek!
3:45pm

 KingofSlack@ClaireRBear Not all of us can be blessed with your wit and charm. Some of us have to make up by overcompensating with the geeky stuff.
3:46pm

 ClaireRBear@KingofSlack There are girls out there who like geeks you know.
3:47pm

 KingofSlack@ClaireRBear Feel free to send them my way. U know where to find me. I'll be finishing up another blog in comp lab
4:00pm

Lots0love Please describe in 140 characters or less why anyone cares about the diff between micro and macro economics

7:09pm

 WiseOneWP@Lots0love I could probably help you out with that if you are serious.

7:11pm

 Lots0love@WiseOneWP It may come to that.

7:13pm

 ClaireRBear@WiseOneWP What was the deal with Benn today? He kept rambling on about imposters? Fakers?

7:30pm

 WiseOneWP@ClaireRBear Oh, that. It's nothing. He and I were just talking about Kirk and Spock last night and um, yeah, must have inspired him

7:34pm

 ClaireRBear@WiseOneWP Because Spock lied to Kirk?

7:35pm

 WiseOneWP@ClaireRBear Not exactly, but I mean, Spock did pretend to be more human than he was to try and fit in . . . at first.

7:38pm

 WiseOneWP@ClaireRBear And in doing so unintentionally hurt people and himself.

7:40pm

155

ClaireRBear@WiseOneWP You are making my head hurt. Enough Star Trek analysis! I have enough drama in my own life.
7:41pm

 WiseOneWP@ClaireRBear Drama?
7:43pm

 ClaireRBear@WiseOneWP I can't believe I forgot to fill you in! You know how JD had been tweeting me? Well we had this convo after concert
7:44pm

 ClaireRBear@WiseOneWP because he was really weird when I talked to him that night. Remember? Anyway, we've talked some more since.
7:45pm

 ClaireRBear@WiseOneWP You know what's super funny? Your name came up one night.
7:46pm

 ClaireRBear@WiseOneWP He seemed a little jealous of you or something! IDK. Maybe he thought we were dating?
7:50pm

 WiseOneWP@ClaireRBear Really? That would be hilarious.
7:55pm

 ClaireRBear@WiseOneWP I told him you and I were just friends so it's all good. And then right before dinner, he called and asked what I was up to tmrw.
7:59pm

ClaireRBear@WiseOneWP We're going to catch a movie!! I haven't even told Lottie yet!

8:00pm

 WiseOneWP@ClaireRBear You mean he asked you out?? Wow. Wow. That is great Claire. Really great.

8:01pm

 WiseOneWP@ClaireRBear Listen. Gotta run. See you tmrw! Um, yeah. Bye!

8:03pm

 Lots0love Oh cruel universe, why do you have to fling the Fling in my face with no date secured?

8:15pm

 ClaireRBear@Lots0love Cheer up buttercup. I'm sure you will find someone fab. You always do.

8:20pm

 ClaireRBear@Lots0love What about John Walker? Thought that was going well.

8:23pm

 Lots0love@ClaireRBear Still working on it. Seems to be taking more time than I had anticipated.

8:30pm

KingofSlack You are gifted. *RT@ClaireRBear I'm sure you will find someone fab. You always do.*

8:31pm

 ClaireRBear@Lots0love PS: Have news to share. Meet me at Sit n Sip before school tmrw!!

8:35pm

 Lots0love@ClaireRBear News? You want me to wait till tmrw for news? That's so cruel!

8:37pm

 Lots0love@ClaireRBear Fine. Guess I'll have to suffer through until then. See ya there. xxoo

9:05pm

ClaireRBear Just filled my girl in on the big news of the day. Woo-hoo!

Thursday, April 1, 7:56am

Lots0love@ClaireRBear Woo-hoo is right!! I'd add a yippee to that as well!

7:57am

KingofSlack Why does everyone get so hot and bothered by the idea of Spring Fling? It's a dance. You dance. Then you go home. La dee da.

7:57am

Lots0love@KingofSlack Oh. Is somebody upset because they might not get to go this year?

8:01am

WiseOneWP@KingofSlack JD asked Claire out. On an actual date.

8:03am

KingofSlack@WiseOneWP Seriously? No, you're messing with me. This is an April Fool's joke.

8:05am

WiseOneWP@KingofSlack THIS IS NOT AN APRIL FOOL'S JOKE!! MY LIFE IS THE JOKE!

8:08am

KingofSlack@WiseOneWP Didn't see that one coming so fast.

8:09am

WiseOneWP@KingofSlack You didn't? Oh, because I totally did. It was actually my plan all along to set her up with the best-looking guy in school so I'd stand zero chance whatsoever.
8:09am

 KingofSlack@WiseOneWP Well then congrats. Job well done.
8:10am

 WiseOneWP@KingofSlack Oh shut up! Why does Claire feel the need to tell ME this stuff?
8:11am

 WiseOneWP@KingofSlack Doesn't she have Lottie for that girl-talk stuff?
8:11am

 KingofSlack@WiseOneWP On the bright side, she's still talking to u.
8:12am

 WiseOneWP I realize today is **#AprilFools**, but why does it feel like the joke is on me?
8:15am

 WiseOneWP I've had too much tweeting for one day. I'm out of here.
8:45am

Lots0love Too much school = need for party this weekend. Heard rumblings. Keep us posted people.
12:17pm

 Lots0love@ClaireRBear You in?
12:20pm

 ClaireRBear@Lots0love If the occasion presents itself, I might be persuaded to go.
12:23pm

 Lots0love@ClaireRBear That's my girl. You still feeling all bubbly and happy and ready for your big date tonight?
5:02pm

 ClaireRBear@Lots0love I'm trying to stay bubbly for sure. But super nervous! What if he doesn't like me?
5:03pm

 Lots0love@ClaireRBear Don't be silly. He asked YOU out. He obviously likes you. Remember, if boys were easy to understand, they wouldn't be as much fun.
5:05pm

 ClaireRBear@Lots0love You know what's odd? Now that he is talking to me at school, I never hear from him on Twitter. He was kinda sweet in tweets.
5:08pm

161

Lots0love@ClaireRBear Do you really want to go back to when he didn't talk to u in person? And nothing is stopping u from still tweeting him.
5:15pm

 ClaireRBear@Lots0love I know. Guess you are right. Better this way. Enough about me. Any progress with John?
5:28pm

 Lots0love@ClaireRBear Things are moving along quite smoothly now thank you very much.
5:29pm

 ClaireRBear@Lots0love Glad to hear it. Yeah, you're probably right. I have to run and prep. Talk l8tr.
5:40pm

 Lots0love@ClaireRBear GOOD LUCK! And just have fun!! xoxo
6:00pm

 Lots0love@KingofSlack Hey Slacker. Don't judge, but was reading some of your old posts. Seem tense. What happened? Did big Benn get in over his head?
6:01pm

 KingofSlack@Lots0love You are such a sweetie. Really. I'm sure the Jr. League can't wait to have you.
6:04pm

 Lots0love@KingofSlack They are knocking now actually. But seriously, what was up with that one crazy post about wolves? Who is the wolf??
6:05pm

KingofSlack@Lots0love It was stupid. Didn't know what to write so just made something up.
6:10pm

 Lots0love@KingofSlack Sure big guy. You positive the sad and overlooked prince charming isn't you?
6:13pm

 KingofSlack@Lots0love You only wish you could find out.
6:23pm

 Lots0love@KingofSlack Not for all the money in the world. I'm out. Have a lax meeting.
6:24pm

 KingofSlack@Lots0love Say hi to the jocks for me. I'm sure they miss me loads.
7:00pm

 ClaireRBear Night y'all. I'm off for my big ole date!
7:31pm

WiseOneWP Up late and pretending to study. Too much on mind.

10:39pm

 ClaireRBear Why does my best friend always pick the big nights to go to sleep early?

10:40pm

 ClaireRBear@WiseOneWP Hey! You're up too! Have time to talk?

10:42pm

 WiseOneWP@ClaireRBear Sure. Saw you were getting ready for your date. How'd it go?

10:45pm

 ClaireRBear@WiseOneWP Forgot I had posted that. Was a little punch drunk earlier.

10:45pm

 WiseOneWP@ClaireRBear So, you still punch drunk now? Kind of late to be getting home from your date. Mom not mad?

10:46pm

 ClaireRBear@WiseOneWP She's a little upset, but then she kind of eased up. Not every day her little girl goes on dates, you know.

10:47pm

 WiseOneWP@ClaireRBear You could go on dates all the time if you weren't so hung up on JD. So was Mr. Perfect everything you dreamed he would be?

10:48pm

ClaireRBear@WiseOneWP He was fine.
10:48pm

 WiseOneWP@ClaireRBear Fine? That's all I get?
10:48pm

 ClaireRBear@WiseOneWP I guess just not what I expected.
10:49pm

 ClaireRBear@WiseOneWP I mean, he picked me up on time and took me to see that new rom-com. So bonus points there.
10:51pm

 ClaireRBear@WiseOneWP Although he drives a massive truck. You should have seen me trying to get in. He literally had to pick me up!
10:51pm

 WiseOneWP@ClaireRBear He picked you up? To put you in his truck? That is uh, nice of him. And strong.
10:53pm

 ClaireRBear@WiseOneWP I know, right? Anyway, we went to dinner after and it was sort of awkward because . . .
10:55pm

 ClaireRBear@WiseOneWP This is going to sound funny . . . he's smarter when he writes than when he talks
11:00pm

WiseOneWP@ClaireRBear You don't say.
11:01pm

 ClaireRBear@WiseOneWP Yeah, totally strange.
11:02pm

 ClaireRBear@WiseOneWP Like, just for example, I was talking about this show on History Channel
11:02pm

 ClaireRBear@WiseOneWP You know the one that shows what the world looks like years from now?
11:03pm

 WiseOneWP@ClaireRBear Love that one. The buildings all crumbly and wild.
11:04pm

 ClaireRBear@WiseOneWP Exactly! And HE said he "didn't like real stuff," his favorite show is For Love of Ray J. Which, I pointed out, is technically "real."
11:05pm

 ClaireRBear@WiseOneWP His other favorite channel is ESPN. He spent 20 mins doing imitations of the announcers. Guess that is the journalism he meant.
11:06pm

 ClaireRBear@WiseOneWP It was probably just nerves. I mean, I was a wreck so I'm sure I wasn't much fun to talk to.
11:07pm

WiseOneWP@ClaireRBear You are always fun to talk to, Claire. Even when you're nervous. You just get sillier is all.

11:09pm

 ClaireRBear@WiseOneWP Um, thanks?

11:10pm

 WiseOneWP@ClaireRBear So that was it? Took you home? Didn't make a move?

11:10pm

 ClaireRBear@WiseOneWP Well, he kind of did. Or I mean, he tried to. Oh God, it was SO embarrassing.

11:11pm

 WiseOneWP@ClaireRBear If too embarrassing, you don't have to tell me about it. Honestly. Forget I asked.

11:13pm

 ClaireRBear@WiseOneWP It's just that, well, when he went to kiss me, I got all flustered and well, I sort of maybe . . . stuck out my hand.

11:15pm

 ClaireRBear@WiseOneWP Like I was going to shake his. Ack! It was so humiliating. He's never going to ask me out again, is he?

11:17pm

 WiseOneWP@ClaireRBear I'm sure it wasn't that bad. Do you WANT to go out with him again?

11:20pm

ClaireRBear@WiseOneWP Sure, if you think that nuclear war isn't "that bad." I think I do though. Want to see if he warms up.
11:21pm

 ClaireRBear@WiseOneWP It just doesn't make sense that he's so sweet on Twitter and so dull in person.
11:22pm

 ClaireRBear@WiseOneWP I'm totally wiped. Thanks for listening. See you tmrw?
11:25pm

 ClaireRBear Night strange and confusing world.
11:30pm

 KingofSlack Day two of all-night attempt to beat my little brother's high score. This is verging on pathetic.
Friday, April 2,12:05am

 KingofSlack HALLELUJAH! I did it! Eat that, baby bro. Now must sleep. But thumbs still twitching.
1:46am

From: **LottieM17@gmail.com**
Sent: Friday, April 2, 6:46am
To: ClaireBearR16@gmail.com
Subject: YEAH!

I'm so sorry I wasn't up to chat with you last night when you got home from big date, but got your message. Yay!! Sounds like you had fun, right? How could you NOT have had fun? You rambled about some awkward kiss thing. Did he kiss you?? I want details ASAP!.

Not to get preachy, but you HAVE to keep playing it cool. I know, it is completely obvious, but the obvious is usually obvious for a reason. The point is, when you see him tomorrow, keep the ball in your court. Think of yourself as the goalie. You do not want him to duck past the defense and slip in and score a direct hit to your heart. You need to deflect, deflect, deflect until you have enough of a lead that a few hits to the heart won't hurt. Does this make any sense? Basically you need to make sure that you do not do what every other girl at WP has done with Jack Whitcomb—become a bumbling fool when he enters the room. You are smart, quirky, talented, adorable, and his talking to you does not make you a better person. It makes HIM

a better person for hanging with you. You do NOT
need to go all ga-ga just b/c he might ask you to
Fling. Let him be the one to keep chasing you.
Guys LOVE the chase—almost as much as I do.

Love ya,
Lottie

ClaireRBear I can't believe I forgot April Fool's Day! It's my fave holiday!
11:43am

 KingofSlack Aliens spotted outside Chick-fil-A. Word is they have searched entire galaxy for the perfect nugget.
11:49am

 LotsOlove Not a big fan of a day that glorifies lies. Aliens? Come on!
11:51am

 KingofSlack@LotsOlove It's not April Fool's anymore, Miss Knows Lots.
11:51am

 ClaireRBear@KingofSlack Remember April Fool's when we were 11? You convinced Beth MacGill aliens really HAD invaded?
11:55am

 KingofSlack@ClaireRBear How could I forget? Don't tell Will, but I'm pretty sure I had him convinced too.
11:57am

 ClaireRBear@KingofSlack My lips are sealed!
11:57am

 LotsOlove With no real solid potentials on the horizon, thinking of going stag to Fling. That would be new.
12:05pm

 ClaireRBear@LotsOlove You know you will get a date. With John—or whoever. Then we can double! I hope!!
12:07pm

Lots0love@ClaireRBear I think YOU, lady, are definitely going. At least that was what message sounded like . . .

12:10pm

 ClaireRBear@Lots0love Sorry I didn't get to properly fill you in yet today. Was running to math quiz when I saw you earlier.

12:11pm

 ClaireRBear@Lots0love Basically, it was sort of fun, sort of weird. G-night kiss was a bit of a train wreck. Stopped before it started.

12:11pm

 ClaireRBear@Lots0love Still, I saw him in hall earlier and he asked me about going to Charlie's party this weekend

12:12pm

 Lots0love@ClaireRBear So I take it you'll have to wait till party for that perfect first kiss?

12:15pm

 ClaireRBear@Lots0love I guess so. I hope it isn't as awkward this time. Or dull.

12:18pm

 ClaireRBear@Lots0love I just wish he would talk to me the way he did online.

12:20pm

 Lots0love@ClaireRBear Well he is a guy. Guys aren't always good talkers face to face.

12:30pm

ClaireRBear@Lots0love Will is a guy and he is good at talking.
12:31pm

 Lots0love@ClaireRBear But is he as hot as JD? You crushing on Will now Bear?
12:32pm

 ClaireRBear@Lots0love I'm just pointing out that he is capable of conversation. And it is not like Will isn't cute!
12:34pm

 Lots0love@ClaireRBear Okay, okay. If you say so.
12:45pm

 ClaireRBear@Lots0love You are impossible. Need to get to class. Talk later.
12:51pm

 KingofSlack Newest blog post is up for cyber world to read.
1:01pm

 WiseOneWP No sleep last night. Glad other people are cheery.
1:03pm

BIG MOUTH B

Thank you for being a friend, or at least not ignoring me in the hallway.

Friday, April 2, 1:00pm

Time for more lessons on surviving school from the man with the big mouth. So we have covered girls (a little—trust me, I'll have more on that subject later) and now let us move on to friends. Friends are the glue that keeps us all here. Without them, who would drive you to school or skip class with you when you need to pick up a new pair of sneaks because you stepped in dog crap on the way onto campus? Boy or girl, upperclassman or underclassman, we all need our friends—just like the cheesy songs tell us. What follows are thoughts on three classic types of high school friendships: the best friend, the girl friend (not the girlfriend you make out with but the girl friend who you get advice from), and the frenemy. If you have more than this many friends, power to you.

1) The best friend: This is your buddy till the end. He will help you get those new sneaks, or just hang out with you for hours while you clean the basement because apparently you are being punished for leaving food down there during your marathon Halo sessions. With this friend you must ALWAYS pay it back—when he finds himself in way over his head,

be there for him, just like you were there freshman year after he partook of one too many Mike's Hard Lemonades and spent the evening throwing up on your couch—and you. Note: I'm still waiting for that replacement shirt my friend—you KNOW what I'm talking about.

2) The Girl Friend: If you are lucky enough to have made it into high school while retaining a friend of the opposite sex, DO NOT LET HER GO! This friend will not only keep you from becoming a total and utter shut-in — she will provide you with advice if the day ever comes that you find yourself wanting a girlfriend. I would advise, however, that said girl who is just a friend, be at least a little bit more socially confident than you are. Otherwise you'll probably just both be losers. Luckily for me, my girl buddy seems to be on the road to Popularville, so perhaps there is hope for me yet. Although . . . anyway, that is for another post.

Finally, 3) The Frenemy: This is the person with whom, through unfortunate circumstances, you've been thrown into the same crowd or sphere. You circle each other like sharks, biting occasionally, but keeping the peace for the benefit of others. This type of friendship is the hardest to understand because it straddles a very fine line between love and hate. Makes you wonder, which side would you rather settle on permanently? One of these days, you might have to decide.

That's it for this morning. Go forth and prosper, my minions.

ClaireRBear It is spring!! So why are teachers giving us so many last minute assignments!?
3:45pm

 ClaireRBear Note to self. Do not pursue career in chemistry. Bombed that one!
3:53pm

 Lots0love Why focus on that when there is a party to look forward to? *RT@ClaireRBear Bombed that one!*
4:00pm

 ClaireRBear I'm not going to stress over the little things . . . like grades and future.
4:02pm

 Lots0love Love the sarcasm. *RT@ClaireRBear I'm not going to stress over the little things . . . like grades and future.*
4:04pm

WiseOneWP So much to do, so much to say, so screwed. Why did I do this to myself?
4:20pm

 KingofSlack I like to keep my two personalities totally separate. Like the superheroes do. Like Clark Kent and Superman.
4:22pm

 WiseOneWP Believes his best friend is suffering from multi-personality disorder. Is this something the school nurse can handle?
4:33pm

 KingofSlack Mock all you want, but there is something awesome about leading a double life. That's why superheroes rock so hard.
4:35pm

 WiseOneWP@KingofSlack I'm not so sure that it is all that great. It can get you pretty messed up . . .
4:38pm

 KingofSlack@WiseOneWP Well you would probably know better than any of us.
4:40pm

 WiseOneWP@KingofSlack Now I have to finish article for next week's edition. Sports page won't write itself
4:41pm

KingofSlack Still think it's hilarious that most unathletic guy at school edits sports section. *RT@WiseOne SportsWP page won't write itself*
4:42pm

 ClaireRBear I really should motivate to start writing too but not in mood to advise.
4:50pm

 ClaireRBear@WiseOneWP So I've been thinking I might have been too quick to judge JD. We had some pretty great tweets . . .
4:52pm

 ClaireRBear@WiseOneWP We talked about movies and life and stuff. It was more than just flirting. I'd be mean to just brush him off after one date.
4:53pm

 ClaireRBear@WiseOneWP You kind of remind me of him actually. I mean, not a lot, but there are little things.
4:56pm

 WiseOneWP@ClaireRBear I'm sure you mean b/c we are both good looking and charming
4:56pm

 ClaireRBear@WiseOneWP That's it! Not the good looking part but the sort of off-beat sense of humor. Funny.
4:59pm

WiseOneWP@ClaireRBear Are you saying I'm not good looking? You know you've wanted me since you saw me in that Tarzan costume when I was six.
5:03pm

 ClaireRBear@WiseOneWP You caught me. Well, now that that secret is out . . .
5:05pm

 WiseOneWP@ClaireRBear I guess I'll just have to wait till you tire of JD and come crawling back
5:07pm

 ClaireRBear@WiseOneWP If that ever happens, you'll totally be my rebound guy.
5:10pm

 ClaireRBear@WiseOneWP Okay, should really go say hi to Maverick. Thanks as always. You're a pal!
5:11pm

 WiseOneWP@KingofSlack DUDE!!! Why doesn't she get that the guy she likes is really me?
5:57pm

 KingofSlack@WiseOneWP Hmm. Maybe because you LIED to her?
6:03pm

 WiseOneWP@KingofSlack Right. Thanks for the reminder.
6:05pm

WiseOneWP@KingofSlack I just need JD to stop hanging out with her. He will, right?

6:08pm

 KingofSlack@WiseOneWP Not sure that is going to happen. Everybody is talking about him taking her to Charlie's party tomorrow. Everybody.

6:30pm

 WiseOneWP@KingofSlack Great, just great.

6:37pm

 KingofSlack@WiseOneWP Look on the bright side. This gives you a chance to go out and pretend to be a happy, well socialized high schooler.

6:38pm

 WiseOneWP@KingofSlack So says the guy who thinks parties are supposed to be like the ones in lame teen movies. You're not EVER going to crowd surf, B. Or sing in a rock band.

6:39pm

 KingofSlack@WiseOneWP Dude, just cause UR pissed, don't be hating. I'm out. Go wallow by yourself.

6:41pm

BIG MOUTH B

We all need to loosen up . . . to make our parents feel successful . . .

Saturday, April 3, 2:15pm

I'm writing with an urgent and important message. Consider this a PSA. An early warning alarm system set in place like those annoying tornado sirens that they have down in the deep South (you know, like Tennessee).

It has come to my attention that the students of WP upper school are strung way too tight. It's spring! We are supposed to be relaxing. Enjoying the allergen-filled air. Skipping classes. Wearing skimpy clothing (Girls—this was directed at you. No offense, fellas, but I got no desire to see your pale and pasty legs). Instead, everyone is hunched over their assigned desks in the library, frantically typing away to meet unrealistic deadlines placed upon us by cruel teachers.

But don't you see—it is all a big conspiracy. The only reason that teachers give us these assignments is to ensure that the product they have been grooming for all these years (namely us, the students) will get into the Ivies, which will make WP look good. In turn, our parents pressure us to keep working, to remember that colleges can revoke admittance if your grades drop. They remind us that a well-rounded student is the ONLY kind of student there should be. Because for our parents, the better school we get into, the better they look. You see how this all works? Is it becoming clearer? Has the PSA message gone through?

You can either go back to your books and ignore my plea to open your eyes or you can take my path. A path I worked hard to clear—namely that of doing nothing. This is the perfect antidote. While you are struggling to put the finishing touches on your senior projects or your oral presentation for history, I am here, blogging—which is, at its core, a procrastination tool. And I do this because I have seen the light and I refuse to allow my parents to live vicariously through me. I will find my own successes . . . eventually.

So I say, rise up now. Say no to the man! And if you are too programmed to say no on a more permanent basis, then just relax for the weekend. Get out and play. Do something scandalous like drive your car on an empty tank or talk to a geek you might see in the hall or hit up a party at Charlie's house (Steph—see you there?). But whatever you do, remember—defy the rents!

Lots0love Countdown to fun has begun. Got the music going, the makeup out, and the outfit picked.
Saturday, April 3, 5:39pm

 ClaireRBear A whole bunch of answers up on Get Clueless blog. Apparently Get Clueless got a lot of time on her hands. http://tiny.cc/GyGa5
5:39pm

 KingofSlack Which shirt to wear tonight? Rock it old school with a gun show T-shirt or classic with button down? **#itsaparty**
5:39pm

 WiseOneWP Wish my problems were as minor as what T-shirt to pick out.
5:47pm

 KingofSlack Bro, picking pants is not something to get all worked up over.
5:50pm

 WiseOneWP@KingofSlack Why are you so persistently charming? *RT@KingofSlack Bro, picking pants is not something to get all worked up over.*
6:00pm

 Lots0love@ClaireRBear You all ready Bear? You're wearing outfit we picked, right? When is JD picking you up?
7:29pm

 ClaireRBear@Lots0love He said he'd be by around 8:30. So you'll be there when I get there right?
7:31pm

Lots0love@ClaireRBear Of course! You'll be fine. Just have fun, relax, and enjoy the ride!
7:34pm

 ClaireRBear@Lots0love I'll try. Let's just hope I don't shake his hand again tonight. I have to kiss him!
7:35pm

 Lots0love@ClaireRBear I don't imagine he'll have any objections. See you there B! Wish me luck with John!! Need to lock down date.
7:36pm

 KingofSlack I'm looking mighty fine if I do say so myself. Watch out ladies.
7:40pm

 Lots0love@KingofSlack Loser
7:41pm

 KingofSlack@Lots0love Wow, that is the sweetest thing you've ever said to me. Thanks Lots.
7:42pm

WiseOneWP Why did I let myself get talked into going out? No fun. Girls got too drunk. Guys put on attitude. No one actually talked . . .

Sunday, April 4, 10:11am

 Lots0love Once again wondering why my parents have not caved and bought me the vehicle I require. It's cramping my style—and keeping me locked in house.

10:21am

 Lots0love Aha! Sneaky rents, now I see your plan.

10:22am

 Lots0love@ClaireRBear Hello darling girl. You have fun last night? Am I mistaken, or did I see you being all cuddly with JD?

10:23am

 ClaireRBear@Lots0love I had fun. Just confused by boys. They're all difficult. Well maybe not Erik Northman. But he is a vampire, not real boy.

10:40am

 Lots0love@ClaireRBear Whoa. Hold up. What is going on? What happened last night?

10:41am

 ClaireRBear@Lots0love If you hadn't abandoned me for John Walker you would have known already . . .

10:43am

 Lots0love@ClaireRBear Ouch. If you were really upset, you could have interrupted me you know.

10:44am

ClaireRBear@Lots0love I'm sorry. That was harsh.
10:45am

 Lots0love@ClaireRBear Apology accepted. So tell me now what's going on? I would totally come over but folks are out, and as always I'm without a car.
10:47am

 ClaireRBear@Lots0love Nothing is really going on. I did have fun. Sort of. I tried to. I really WANTED to.
10:47am

 Lots0love@ClaireRBear It certainly looked like you were having fun . . .
10:51am

 ClaireRBear@Lots0love We didn't make out if that is what you are implying. We got close but to be honest, I didn't want to.
11:01am

 Lots0love@ClaireRBear Please explain.
11:01am

 ClaireRBear@Lots0love Well, I think JD isn't quite the guy I thought he was. If that makes any sense.
11:04am

 ClaireRBear@Lots0love I mean, I'm just not into him as much as I thought I would be. Don't get me wrong, he's hot, but . . .
11:05am

Lots0love@ClaireRBear So that is it? You are over him? Just like that?
11:06am

ClaireRBear@Lots0love I didn't say that. It's just, well, he's kind of dull.
11:07am

 Lots0love@ClaireRBear Blasphemy!!
11:10am

 ClaireRBear@Lots0love I thought maybe that would change once we went out again but all he talked about was lacrosse.
11:11am

 ClaireRBear@Lots0love And he told me the EXACT same story he told me on Thursday!
11:12am

  Lots0love@ClaireRBear Maybe he doesn't have a good memory. But he was talking to you! Isn't that what you wanted?
11:19am

 ClaireRBear@Lots0love I want to talk WITH someone, not be talked at BY someone.
11:21am

 ClaireRBear@Lots0love IDK. I'm just not as into him as I once was.
11:22am

 ClaireRBear@Lots0love Anyway, distract me—did you hook up with John?
11:23am

Lots0love@ClaireRBear I'll fill you in on all the gory details when I see you. Gotta run. Mom's back and wants to go shopping. Later.
11:40am

ClaireRBear Seriously folks, another trending topic about **#jonasbrothers**? I think perhaps there are better ways to use your—and my—time.

11:59am

 ClaireRBear Time is tick, tick, ticking away. And now my mother is locked in the den again with her cyber love affair.

1:04pm

 ClaireRBear Sigh.

1:07pm

Lots0love Ready for school to be over! Only a little over month left. With fling in between! Hope I get flung!
Monday, April 5, 7:09am

 KingofSlack Anyone found a way to time travel?
7:10am

 ClaireRBear Going to be positive. The sun is shining, birds are chirping, and if this were a movie, people would be breaking into song.
7:30am

 ClaireRBear@Lots0love Just saw JD in hall on way to free period. He asked me to Fling!!
9:02am

 Lots0love@ClaireRBear What did you say?? You said yes, right? You had to have said yes.
9:03am

 ClaireRBear@Lots0love I told him I'd think about it.
9:09am

 Lots0love@ClaireRBear Excuse me? What is there to think about?
9:10am

 Lots0love@ClaireRBear The whole personality thing can be worked on!
9:11am

ClaireRBear@Lots0love Rather not have to work that hard. If he has nothing interesting to say now, what's going to be left to talk about in a month?
9:12am

 ClaireRBear@Lots0love Can we go to Chick for lunch today? Think we both need waffle fries
9:13am

 Lots0love@ClaireRBear Definitely . . . and I'll talk some sense into you.
9:14am

 KingofSlack Just saw that there is going to be double chaperone at Fling. Last year got too out of hand is the rumor.
9:14am

 ClaireRBear Free period first thing in the morning is a blessing and a curse. Gotta go catch up on stuff didn't get done over the weekend.
9:16am

 ClaireRBear@Lots0love Scratch Chick today. Study group for math is during lunch. Tmrw?
11:58am

 Lots0love@ClaireRBear Sounds like a plan.
12:01pm

ClaireRBear Math is giving me too many headaches. So did study group. Boo!
1:29pm

 KingofSlack Ever notice that Monday after a party, everyone looks slightly guilty? What did you do WPers? What did you do?
1:31pm

 ClaireRBear@WiseOneWP Hey there, didn't see much of you at the party. Where'd you go?
1:31pm

 WiseOneWP@ClaireRBear You seemed pretty busy. Didn't want to bother you on your big date.
1:34pm

 ClaireRBear@WiseOneWP Knock it off. You know I always like talking to you! Plus, I could have used the distraction
1:35pm

 WiseOneWP@ClaireRBear What do you mean? Looked like you were having fun.
1:35pm

 ClaireRBear@WiseOneWP I think you once told me that looks can be deceiving. Wasn't having that much fun.
1:36pm

 ClaireRBear@WiseOneWP I was kind of bored. JD doesn't have a lot to say. I mean he does, but it is mostly about lax, carolina ball, and oh yeah, lax.
1:37pm

ClaireRBear@WiseOneWP Not much for me to contribute to those conversations. Do you know he has never even heard of Battlestar?
1:38pm

 WiseOneWP@ClaireRBear He didn't know Battlestar?! Loser! Sorry to hear about that though. I know you were really excited.
1:39pm

 ClaireRBear@WiseOneWP It's funny, I'm not as upset as I thought I would be. I kind of feel like, oddly, I deserve more.
1:40pm

 ClaireRBear@WiseOneWP Although, he did ask me to Fling and haven't said yes or no yet. Leaning toward no. What would be the point?
1:41pm

 WiseOneWP@ClaireRBear Look at you being all confident. You are right though. You do deserve more.
1:41pm

 ClaireRBear@WiseOneWP You are a sweetie. Anyway, gotta run. 5th period bell is about to ring. Have a good day and thanks for listening, as usual!
1:42pm

 KingofSlack Heard that the full moon was out over weekend. Perhaps that is the reason for all the crazy behavior going on in the halls of our beloved school.
1:42pm

Lots0love@KingofSlack Wish you had turned into a werewolf and disappeared into the woods.
1:43pm

 KingofSlack@Lots0love Of course you do. I would be even hotter as a werewolf. Don't even try to deny it.
1:44pm

 WiseOneWP@KingofSlack DUDE! I think the problem is going to solve itself. Claire doesn't like the real JD! This could really blow over!!
1:45pm

 KIngofSlack@WiseOneWP Oh buddy, it's sweet to see u living in a dream world. Real sweet.
1:46pm

 WiseOneWP@KingofSlack It's not a dream. It's going to be fine. And I'm going to tell her how I feel about her. Enough pretending.
1:47pm

 KingofSlack I love to listen to the delusions of others.
1:48pm

 Lots0love@KingofSlack You mean your own delusions. *RT@KingofSlack I love to listen to the delusions of others.*
1:48pm

KingofSlack@Lots0love If only you knew. If only you knew.
1:49pm

 ClaireRBear@KingofSlack If only she knew what? It's okay Benn, we won't judge.
2:00pm

 KingofSlack I'm outta here.
2:01pm

WATKINS WEEKLY

Tuesday, April 6, 2010

LET'S TRY SOMETHING NEW . . .

Lately I've been feeling especially clueless in love and life. More so than usual, if that can be believed. So clueless, in fact, that I don't feel much like answering questions from readers who might take my advice too seriously. What if they were to suffer the consequences? It's too much pressure. So for today, I'm letting readers off the hook. I am going to ask myself questions. I will answer them with the use of a Magic 8 Ball, which I figure can't possibly be any more clueless with its responses than I would be. Let's see how it goes.

Dear Magic 8 Ball,
Do you believe in second chances?
—So Very Clueless

The answer is: Outlook not so good.

Hi again, Ball,
Am I going to have the perfect first kiss?
—Still Lacking a Clue

The answer is: Without a doubt.

Well hello, Glossy Orb of Wisdom,
Fancy meeting you here. I'm getting ready to go to a party. What should I wear, skirt or jeans?

—Eternally Clueless

The answer is: It is decidedly so.

Hmm,
Let's try another one, since you are not being particularly helpful with fashion: Does dating get more fun with practice?

—Me Again

The answer is: Cannot predict now.

I'm back, You Useless Chunk of Plastic,
One final question: I'm going to have to figure everything out myself, aren't I? You're not going to help me one little bit, are you?

—Okay Fine, Perhaps Slightly Less
Clueless than Inanimate Objects

The answer is: It is certain.

ClaireRBear@WiseOneWP@KingofSlack Followed by tasty pizza?

9:51am

 KingofSlack@WiseOneWP@ClaireRBear No can do at my place. But why don't you two crazy kids take the party to Claire's?

9:52am

 ClaireRBear Love a plan! See you tonight Will!

9:55am

 WiseOneWP@KingofSlack I'm going to kill you.

9:55am

 KingofSlack@WiseOneWP What William? I was just trying to help a brother out. Wanna grab lunch at Chick? I'm jonesing for a shake and tasty chix sandwich

9:56am

 WiseOneWP@KingofSlack Sure, fine, whatever. Might as well stuff my face before I come face-to-face with Claire

9:57am

ClaireRBear Loving my new system of answering. to the chase is my new motto. What do you all th Let me know at http://tiny.cc/GyGa5

Tuesday, April 6, 9:45am

 KingofSlack Better not tell you now. *RT@ClaireRB What do you all think?*

9:46am

 ClaireRBear@KingofSlack Party pooper. You are ju worried if you write in, I'll answer you with an Outlo not so good.

9:46am

 KingofSlack@WiseOneWP Dude. Any luck with telling you-know-who about you-know-what?

9:47am

 WiseOneWP@KingofSlack Not yet. I don't want to mangle it.

9:48am

 KingofSlack@WiseOneWP You are truly ridonculous.

9:49am

 ClaireRBear@WiseOneWP@KingofSlack Hey — wanna bring the paper work home with us and do marathon writing session in Benn's basement tonight?

9:51am

Lots0love Hands down, Chick is the best. Cannot live without it.
1:34pm

 ClaireRBear Odd feeling. Not the chicken but something else
1:35pm

 WiseOneWP@KingofSlack Crap, crap, crap! Did you see Claire!!?? At Chick!
1:48pm

 WiseOneWP@KingofSlack She saw me talking to JD! What if she gets suspicious?
1:51pm

 KingofSlack@WiseOneWP What's the big deal? It's a free world, you can talk to JD whenever u want. Y would she think anything of it?
1:52pm

 KingofSlack@WiseOneWP Although u are a geek and he is a jock, so I can see why it is an odd mix
1:52pm

 WiseOneWP@KingofSlack Thanks buddy. That's a real help
1:55pm

 KingofSlack@WiseOneWP What compelled you to him, anyway?
1:56pm

WiseOneWP@KingofSlack Argh! I told you already! I didn't go up to him! He came up to me!!
1:57pm

 KingofSlack@WiseOneWP My bad. Was working on the fries. So what does it matter? He just asked if you had any advice on how to woo her, right?
1:58pm

 WiseOneWP@KingofSlack Well he didn't say woo but basically, yeah. He was like "since you got her into me" blah blah blah.
1:59pm

 WiseOneWP@KingofSlack I could have sworn Claire heard him. But she didn't say anything. She and Lottie were walking out.
2:00pm

 KingofSlack@WiseOneWP Dude. Calm down. I'm sure you are fine.
2:01pm

 WiseOneWP Right. I think I am beginning to know what it feels like to be buried alive.
2:02pm

 KingofSlack One more class left and then done for the day. Best combo—lunch followed by free followed by art.
2:02pm

 WiseOneWP Wish I could just go home and sleep
2:03pm

Lots0love Only 3 more lax games left before tournaments begin. Thank God! I need my attention for fling.

7:09pm

 ClaireRBear Still not feeling right. Things are off . . .

7:10pm

 ClaireRBear@WiseOneWP Hey, saw you today in Chick. Why didn't you say hi? And what were you talking to JD about?

7:11pm

 ClaireRBear@WiseOneWP Since when are you all chummy? I heard him say my name.

7:14pm

 WiseOneWP@ClaireRBear Hey, sorry about that. I was in a rush. And oh, yeah, JD was just asking if I knew you well.

7:15pm

 ClaireRBear@WiseOneWP Really? That's bizarre. Why?

7:18pm

 WiseOneWP@ClaireRBear Beats me. Guess maybe he's bummed you said no to the dance. You did, right?

7:19pm

 ClaireRBear@WiseOneWP Um yeah. But like, just a few minutes ago when he called. So why would he have been bummed at lunch?

7:21pm

WiseOneWP@ClaireRBear Maybe he knew you would? I don't know. Listen, I have to go but um, I wanted to talk to you about something.
7:22pm

 ClaireRBear@WiseOneWP Okay. You're acting very strange Will Parker. Guess you aren't coming over?
7:24pm

 WiseOneWP@ClaireRBear Yeah, not tonight. I'm not feeling so hot.
7:26pm

 Claire Bear16@WiseOneWP Okay, well feel better I guess. But I'm around if you change your mind. You can tell me whatever it is you wanted to. Or tweet me.
7:30pm

 WiseOneWP@ClaireRBear We really should talk in person. It's something I should have told you before. I think you are incredible, you know that?
7:35pm

 ClaireRBear@WiseOneWP You are starting to freak me out. Just spit it out! Jeez—you are worse than Bennett trying to lie to his mom!
7:36pm

 WiseOneWP@ClaireRBear I'm making a mess out of this. Let's just meet at Sit n Sip. Tomorrow during B period. You're free, right?
7:37pm

 WiseOneWP@ClaireRBear I was supposed to meet with guidance counselor about this internship at USC journalism school but that can wait. You'll meet me?
7:37pm

ClaireRBear@WiseOneWP Yes, yes. I'll meet you. But you better tell me what's going on Will.
7:40pm

 **WiseOneWP@ClaireRBear** Yes, promise. See you tomorrow.
7:41pm

KingofSlack Despite the waffle fries, burger, and side order of sweet potato fries, still hungry for dins. Wonder what mom has cooking.

7:47pm

 Lots0love Going to lay down on couch and ice my shins and read some Austen. Guess there are worse ways to spend the night.

7:49pm

 WiseOneWP@KingofSlack Claire is totally suspicious. I'm meeting her tmrw to tell her.

7:51pm

 KingofSlack@WiseOneWP I'll believe it when I see it my friend.

7:52pm

Lots0love Scandalous rumors going around. Must get to the bottom of this.

Wednesday, April 7, 8:46am

 Lots0love According to the word on the street, JD got rejected.

8:47am

 Lots0love That is BIG happenings in the halls of WP.

8:48am

 Lots0love@ClaireRBear So, is it true? I heard Jessica talking in the hall and she said you said NO to JD

8:49am

 ClaireRBear@Lots0love You heard right. I was going to tell you last night but then Will was being weird and I felt weird so I just went to bed.

8:49am

 ClaireRBear@Lots0love I couldn't say yes. He called and I was going to. But then he started talking about Carolina's season and . . .

8:50am

 ClaireRBear@Lots0love It's not worth it. Hot or not, I've waited this long to date someone, might as well want to talk to them

8:51am

 Lots0love@ClaireRBear Wow. I guess then I'm happy for you? Although sad we won't be going double to Fling.

8:51am

ClaireRBear@Lots0love We still have next year. Maybe I'll have a new crush by then. Can you believe after all this time, I'm done with JD?
8:52am

 Lots0love@ClaireRBear I know that feeling. They never seem to live up to the expectations. The search is all about finding the one who will.
8:53am

 ClaireRBear@Lots0love You know what's funny? I never understood that before but now I kinda get your logic.
8:53am

 ClaireRBear@Lots0love You know what else? I sort of have been thinking about Will a lot. Like he could be the one. But then . . .
8:54am

 ClaireRBear@Lots0love He was so weird last night. I keep thinking about him talking to JD. And there are these other little things that are sort of odd.
8:54am

 ClaireRBear@Lots0love I'm probably being crazy. But like, JD didn't know about some of the stuff we tweeted about.
8:54am

 ClaireRBear@Lots0love And he never once mentioned journalism.
8:55am

ClaireRBear@Lots0love And Will, not JD, is the one into journalism and old movies. It's just strange b/c that is so not JD in real life.
8:56am

 Lots0love@ClaireRBear What are you talking about?
8:56am

 ClaireRBear@Lots0love IDK! Something is just fishy. Whatevs. I gotta get to class and then I'm meeting Will later. I'm sure it is nothing.
8:57am

 KingofSlack The interwebz is all atwitter! News this big even goes beyond the walls of our school. JD Whitcomb DENIED. But not for long?
9:00am

 WiseOneWP One more hour. Just one more hour.
9:01am

 Lots0love@KingofSlack Will is freaking Claire out. Do you know anything about this?
9:02am

 KingofSlack@Lots0love I have no idea what goes through that boy's head. Sorry. Guess you'll just have to wait and see.
9:02am

BIG MOUTH B

Friends don't let friends make fools of themselves . . . most of the time.

Wednesday, April 7, 9:28am

I find myself in a bit of a pickle. Yes, a pickle. (Thanks Grandpop Jones for passing that gem of an expression on to me!) I have learned the sad truth—even the best of intentions can end badly. I know there are some disbelievers out there so I will just list a few examples:

1) Nelson Mandela—so things didn't end badly, but it sure took a while and I imagine being imprisoned all those years was no walk in the park.

2) Joan of Arc—I'm a little iffy on her, but I know that she didn't get no respect till she was dead. Little too late in my opinion.

3) Gandhi—he literally starved himself for his beliefs. Have you seen pics of that dude? Wish someone would have brought him a big ole order of waffle fries. And maybe a bulletproof vest.

4) Martin Luther King, Jr.—One word . . . assassinated. I'm seeing a theme here.

5) Sarah Connor—Bore the child who would save the world from destruction and STILL had to deal with two different versions of Terminators (if you don't count the TV show, which was so rudely canceled!).

Now I know what you are thinking. These people are true heroes. We are just high schoolers. But I would argue that I think the idea can apply to people we walk these very halls with. People who, out of a confused desire to "save" someone, wind up getting hurt themselves. And if the aforementioned people all met rather horrible ends or suffered greatly for their beliefs and they were doing it all for a much larger purpose than love of a girl, I fear that those of us with simpler ideals will have double the pain and punishment (although I think Joan of Arc was burned alive. On a stake. So maybe not).

So to all of you out there on simple but vital missions, best of luck. Wish I could say it will end well . . . but hey, you've seen what happens.

ClaireRBear In state of shock.
8:39pm

 ClaireRBear I cannot believe I have been such a giant fool. I'm the biggest of the giant fools.
8:40pm

 ClaireRBear The signs were all there. Why did I not see them? They could have been written on a JumboTron they were so obvious.
8:41pm

 ClaireRBear Just went through everything in my head. Yup. Signs. Lots and lots of signs.
8:42pm

 ClaireRBear Old movies, sense of humor, intelligent on one hand. Reality tv, dull, self-absorbed on the other.
8:50pm

 ClaireRBear How could I have been so completely and horribly stupid? No, I take that back, how could I be friends with someone so mean?
8:51pm

 ClaireRBear Why would someone do this to someone they care about?
8:55pm

 Lots0love What is going on? *RT@ClaireRBear In state of shock.*
9:00pm

ClaireRBear@Lots0love Did you know??
9:05pm

 Lots0love@ClaireRBear Did I know what?
9:06pm

 ClaireRBear@Lots0love Did you know that all that time that JD was tweeting me it WASN'T JD?
9:08pm

 Lots0love@ClaireRBear What are you talking about? Who was it?
9:09pm

 ClaireRBear@Lots0love It was freaking Will "I'm a huge jerk with stupid hair" Parker! HE was Top of Game. JD was never on Twitter. At least not with me.
9:10pm

 ClaireRBear@Lots0love No wonder the real JD sounded nothing like the one I talked to. I TOLD you something was up!
9:11pm

 Lots0love@ClaireRBear Are you serious?? Why would he do that? He had nothing to do with JD asking you out, right?
9:12pm

 ClaireRBear@Lots0love I don't think so. I mean, I don't really know. I don't know anything anymore.
9:14pm

Lots0love@ClaireRBear Oh Bear, I'm so so sorry. I'm coming over. Right now. Hang in there.
9:15pm

 Lots0love Boys really are jerks. We should throw rocks at them.
9:16pm

 KingofSlack Oh boy. *RT@ClaireRBear In state of shock*
9:17pm

ClaireRBear Friend needs to get here right now!
9:18pm

 ClaireRBear You know when you are so mad that you literally start seeing stars? I'm seeing a freaking galaxy.
9:18pm

 WiseOneWP@ClaireRBear I take it this wouldn't be a good time to say sorry again.
9:20pm

 ClaireRBear@WiseOneWP How can sorry make something like this go away?
9:21pm

 WiseOneWP@ClaireRBear I honestly meant to only do it once. Bennett thought it would be a good way to make you happy.
9:22pm

 ClaireRBear@WiseOneWP Oh, BENNETT thought. Bennett thinks he was abducted by aliens. Why would you listen to him??
9:23pm

 ClaireRBear@WiseOneWP I can't believe he was in on it too. I feel like a complete idiot.
9:24pm

 WiseOneWP@ClaireRBear Please stop. It hurts to see you like this.
9:25pm

WiseOneWP@ClaireRBear It wasn't all lies. I mean, yes, I pretended to be JD but what I was saying as him wasn't made up. That was all me.

9:27pm

 WiseOneWP@ClaireRBear So, hey, on the bright side, the person you liked was me, and I like you back, so it isn't horrible . . .

9:28pm

 ClaireRBear@WiseOneWP You are telling me you like me? Now? Are you for real, Will Parker? I've never been so confused in my entire life.

9:29pm

 ClaireRBear@WiseOneWP You made me judge JD against something MADE UP! I didn't give him a chance because of you.

9:30pm

 ClaireRBear@WiseOneWP It would be only fitting if I called him and asked if he'd still go to fling with me. I won't. But still, don't think I don't want to. Sort of.

9:31pm

 WiseOneWP@ClaireRBear Please, Claire. Let me see you. Once I explain the whole thing and how it got out of control, it might make more sense.

9:32pm

 WiseOneWP@ClaireRBear I tried to tell you. I wanted to tell you so many times but I was scared you'd react just like this.

9:33pm

ClaireRBear@WiseOneWP When Will? When did you try to tell me? When we hung out—like every day? Or how about when I tweeted you—I mean JD??

9:37pm

 ClaireRBear@WiseOneWP Why did you even bother tweeting back???

9:38pm

 WiseOneWP@ClaireRBear I shouldn't have. But I couldn't let you feel like I didn't care.

9:40pm

 ClaireRBear@WiseOneWP You? Or JD? I can't do this, Will. Not right now. I need some time to think about this. About what you did.

9:47pm

 ClaireRBear@WiseOneWP Please. Just give me some space. If you care about me at all.

9:48pm

ClaireRBear It wasn't a bad dream.
Thursday, April 8, 6:45am

 ClaireRBear Please please give me the flu so I can stay home from school.
6:50am

 Lots0love@KingofSlack This pains me to do, but I need to ask you something.
7:45am

 KingofSlack@Lots0love Hello fair Charlotte May. As always, a pleasure to hear from you.
7:48am

 Lots0love@KingofSlack I wanted to hear what you had to say about this whole fiasco involving our friends.
7:49am

 KingofSlack@Lots0love I told Will he shouldn't have done this. Sort of.
7:50am

 Lots0love@KingofSlack So why did he do it?
7:50am

 KingofSlack@Lots0love Honestly? Between u and me? Because he likes her. Haven't u ever done anything crazy for someone u like?
7:51am

216

Lots0love@KingofSlack Have you?
7:52am

 KingofSlack@Lots0love This isn't about me. But I probably would. I think we all do at some point.
7:53am

 KingofSlack@Lots0love He's hurting. He knows he was wrong. For what it's worth.
7:54am

 Lots0love@KingofSlack That probably doesn't matter now. She's heartbroken. And as much as I hate to say it, I don't want her to lose you guys as friends.
7:55am

 KingofSlack@Lots0love I don't want that either. At all. So, what do we do?
7:56am

 Lots0love@KingofSlack WE don't do anything. This is in Will's court. He has to fix this. Do something that will make her see past the hurt.
7:57am

 KingofSlack@Lots0love Like what?
7:58am

 Lots0love@KingofSlack I have absolutely no idea.
8:00am

From: **ParkerWill.2010@gmail.com**
Sent: Thursday, April 8, 9:07am
To: ClaireBearR16@gmail.com
Subject: I'm sorry

Hi Claire,
Since you refuse to text me, tweet me, or speak to me in person or on the phone, I'm hoping that you will at least read this email before you delete it. Even if you don't respond to it.

I am so so sorry. I know those words probably can't begin to ease the pain that I've caused, but I do want you to know that I never intended for it to get so out of hand. It really did start as something simple—even though stupid. I wanted to make you smile. See? Simple. Because when you smile, you light up a room. I know it sounds cheesy, but it's true. Why do you think I signed up to be on the paper—as a *sports* editor? I don't even like sports. I liked—no, I *like,* you. And I was sick of seeing you so sad and fixated on JD Whitcomb. I should have told you the truth.

You said yourself that you deserve better. And you do. You deserve someone who appreciates the fact that when you laugh, you get a dimple in your left cheek, but not your right. Someone who enjoys your tendency to make this odd sort of squeak when you are embarrassed or confused. Someone who looks at you and feels twitterpaited. Like he is the luckiest guy in the world because you are in his life.

Anyway, I should go. Please know that I never meant to hurt you.

—Will P.

_____

From: **ClaireBearR16@gmail.com**
Sent: Thursday, April 8, 4:08pm
To: ParkerWill.2010@gmail.com
Subject: Re: I'm sorry

Will,

I don't really know where to begin. It sounds like you're trying to tell me how much you like me, but I don't understand how a person can treat someone they care about the way you treated me. If you felt that way, you could have said something. Instead, you humiliated me. You made me fall for a guy who didn't even really exist. I don't know which version of you is real. I don't know which version of you I can trust. Or if I can ever trust you again. Until I figure that out, I can't forgive you.

Please don't write me again. Not yet.

—Claire

Lots0love How could things have gone so horribly wrong?
8:56pm

 KingofSlack I'm the one who should be saying told you so. So why do I feel wrong saying it?
9:00pm

 Lots0love My BFF is miserable. It feels like when Serena and Blair had one of their massive fights—minus the good soundtrack.
9:01pm

 KingofSlack@Lots0love They'll make up and have their staircase moment. Just not on the steps of the Met. More like the steps of Sit n Sip or something.
9:02pm

 Lots0love@KingofSlack LOL! You watch GG! Haaaa! Bennett Jones—are you gay?
9:03pm

 KingofSlack@Lots0love I have no shame in loving GG. I'm a straight man who looks to Chuck Bass for inspiration.
9:04pm

 Lots0love@KingofSlack Of course you would look to Chuck. Too bad Will is more the slimy Chuck figure.
9:05pm

 KingofSlack@Lots0love Does that make me the earnest, awkward Dan Humphrey?
9:05pm

Lots0love@KingofSlack Grrr. He makes me so mad!
9:06pm

 KingofSlack@Lots0love Dan Humphrey? What did he ever do to you?
9:07pm

 Lots0love@KingofSlack No! You one-celled organism! WILL makes me mad. Dan just annoys me.
9:07pm

 Lots0love@KingofSlack It's one thing to mess with me, another to mess with Claire. She's a little sweetheart.
9:08pm

 ClaireRBear Ice cream—check. Intentionally sad movie—check. Tissues—check. I'm ready.
9:11pm

 Lots0love@WiseOneWP I am not speaking to you. But before I start not speaking to you, you need to know that if I was speaking to you, I'd tell you to fix this.
9:18pm

 WiseOneWP@Lots0love I'm sorry Lottie. It got out of hand. I emailed her and apologized. I even told her I liked her.
9:20pm

Lots0love@WiseOneWP And you honestly thought that was going to make it all better? You need to get off your butt and go to her house.

9:21pm

 WiseOneWP@Lots0love You're right. But I don't think she'd open the door. Anyway, she's lucky to have a friend like you.

9:25pm

 Lots0love@WiseOneWP Funny, I could have said that about you once, too.

9:30pm

ClaireRBear Ice cream is only a Band-Aid. Pain still there when you wake up.

Friday, April 9, 7:15am

 WiseOneWP@ClaireRBear Are you ever going to talk to me?

7:25am

 ClaireRBear@WiseOneWP Let me check. "My sources say no."

7:26am

 Lots0love@ClaireRBear Wow, you are really giving it to Will.

7:30am

 ClaireRBear@Lots0love Well he deserves it. Wouldn't you? Or would you accept his apology?

7:31am

 Lots0love@ClaireRBear No! Unless you WANT to accept his apology and are being too stubborn to see that maybe he is hurting as much as you.

7:35am

 ClaireRBear@Lots0love I'M being stubborn? That's just priceless. You're starting to sound like Benn.

7:35am

 ClaireRBear@Lots0love Who, I'd like to point out, also hurt me and hasn't even said he was sorry.

7:36am

ClaireRBear@Lots0love I just can't get over how wrong I was about both of them.

7:37am

ClaireRBear@Lots0love I can't forgive Will right now. Or Benn really. Sorry.

7:40am

Lots0love@ClaireRBear Benn's not THAT bad a guy.

7:41am

ClaireRBear It's official. World has gone insane. And still, I have to go to class.

7:58am

Lots0love Sending good vibes to my good friend. Day is halfway over!

12:30pm

KingofSlack Second that emotion. *RT@Lots0love Sending good vibes to my good friend. Day is halfway over!*

12:41pm

WiseOneWP@ClaireRBear I didn't intend to humiliate you. I wanted to make you happy. That's all.

1:01pm

ClaireRBear@WiseOneWP Will. I asked for space.

1:05pm

ClaireRBear@WiseOneWP And IF you liked me, which I'm not even sure you did, I still argue you could have said something.

1:05pm

WiseOneWP@ClaireRBear What would I have said? I was worried things would be ruined forever.
1:06pm

 ClaireRBear@WiseOneWP Well now they are anyway, so a whole lot of good your alternate plan did.
1:08pm

 WiseOneWP@ClaireRBear I wish you would just give me a chance. We could start over. You could come to fling w/me . . .
1:10pm

 ClaireRBear@WiseOneWP You have GOT to be joking. Please understand how I can't do that.
1:11pm

 WiseOneWP@ClaireRBear I understand. But I meant what I said. You make me twitterpated. Always have.
1:15pm

 WiseOneWP@ClaireRBear And if you really want me to leave you alone, I will. I'm sorry Claire.
1:16pm

From: **LottieM17@gmail.com**
Sent: Friday, April 9, 6:24pm
To: BennettJonesEsq@gmail.com
Subject: The apocalypse

Hey Bennett,

Sorry to bug you with an email. I'm sure you are very busy figuring out which mage you want to trade for which dragon or whatever it is you do with your evenings. But I have been thinking long and hard about this whole Claire/Will/fake JD thing. I think, and you have to take this to your grave, that maybe Claire is being just a little too hard on Will.

Don't get me wrong, what he did was completely psycho, but maybe Claire should hear him out. Right before she found out about everything, she was beginning to suspect something was going on and she sort of admitted she liked Will. It wasn't a flat-out declaration but I know my Claire-speak, and she might as well have just spit it out. And more importantly, the idea seemed to make her so happy. So I can't let her just throw it all away, even if I think Will is in for some serious groveling first. She needs to at least hear someone else's version of what happened. Nothing I say is getting through to her. Maybe you could try??

Like it or not, we are stuck in this together. So, are you going to help me save Claire's world from being totally destroyed?

—Lottie

PS: She wants an apology from you too. Don't think you are entirely off the hook. I wasn't going to forgive you either but, well, I need your help. And you tried to stop Will. Right?

From: **BennettJonesEsq@gmail.com**
Sent: Friday, April 9, 7:06pm
To: LottieM17@gmail.com
Subject: Re: The apocalypse

Hey Charlotte,
It is always my first inclination to help someone who begins an email with a total diss. Makes me want to just jump right off my couch, throw down my game console, and get right to work easing your troubles. Luckily, I'm a nice guy despite the jerk persona I try to cultivate (you know it works—the ladies are lined up!) and you actually sound pretty upset.

Will made a mistake. But it came from a good place. And I think Will has learned his lesson: No more creepy online alter egos in the name of love. Not all of us are as wise and flawless as you, Charlotte.

Your humble kicking bag,
Benn

PS. I know. I do owe her an apology. And yes. I did try to stop him.

From: **LottieM17@gmail.com**
Sent: Friday, April 9, 8:02pm
To: BennettJonesEsq@gmail.com
Subject: Thanks

Hey, just wanted to say thanks for talking me off the ledge.
—Lottie
PS. Why do you always call me Charlotte?

From: **BennettJonesEsq@gmail.com**
Sent: Friday, April 9, 7:06pm
To: LottieM17@gmail.com
Subject: Re: Thanks

Lottie is a name for someone who has air for brains. You, Charlotte May, have no air in your brain.

ClaireRBear Thank God for the barn. Maverick will make everything better.

Saturday, April 10, 11:07am

 KingofSlack I've figured it out!! We are being taped for a new reality show. The Hills: Southern Style. That's why people are acting crazy.

11:45am

 LotsOlove Who would you be? The jokester? Or the depressed one who never leaves the couch? *RT@KingofSlack We are being taped for a new reality show.*

11:51am

 KingofSlack@LotsOlove I would be the heartthrob, of course! With my bulging biceps and A&F physique. All my female costars would have catfights over me.

11:56am

 LotsOlove@KingofSlack Don't know why I didn't see it before! Thx for the laff. Needed it today.

12:01pm

 LotsOlove Feeling sort of confused and sad. This is becoming a pattern that I don't like. When did things get so complicated?

12:04pm

 KingofSlack@LotsOlove Ahh . . . does somebody need a hug? Seriously? Like I said, I got a great set of guns . . .

12:05pm

From: **ParkerWill.2010@gmail.com**
Sent: Saturday, April 10, 1:03pm
To: BennettJonesEsq@gmail.com
Subject: Happened anyway

You happy now? You were totally right. I should have stopped sooner. It's just, I don't know, Benn, Claire's amazing. Everytime I see her I have to stop myself from trying to kiss her. Which would be really awkward right now, since she refuses to even look at me.

I wanted to tell her so many times. When she came over that one night and you bailed and we got left alone? It was so great. We just sat there and talked and laughed and I felt like she really got me. And the way she picks at her cuticles when she's nervous—I mean, I know other guys might find that disgusting but it's so cute. I was going to tell her that night, but then we started talking about her dad and she got all teary and all I wanted to do was hug her. What was I supposed to say after that? "Oh yeah, by the way, JD hasn't been tweeting you, I have. Ha ha!" That would go over real well I'm sure.

What do I do, man? My biggest fear has come true. She is gone.

From: **BennettJonesEsq@gmail.com**
Sent: Saturday, April 10, 1:34pm
To: ParkerWill.2010@gmail.com
Subject: I was right

When are you going to learn, my friend? Bennett Jones is all knowing and all wise. Bennett Jones is a prophet of our times. Bennett Jones is going to stop talking in the third person. I'm glad you are man enough to admit I was right to tell you to stop.

Charlotte and I have talked and agree, you have to figure out something big. Huge. Monumental in fact, if you want to get this fixed. What that is, I don't know but you are in it deep, dude. And if you want to make this right, you'll figure out what to do to show Claire how you feel. You, not JD.

—Mr. All-Knowing (that's what you can call me from now on, if you would be so kind)

From: **ClaireBearR16@gmail.com**

Sent: Saturday, April 10, 2:46pm

To: LottieM17@gmail.com

Subject: Make it go away

Oh Lots, please tell me this goes away. This icky feeling. I'll feel better soon, right? I'm so glad you are my best friend. I couldn't have gotten through this without you.

Can I tell you a secret? I know I shouldn't, but I miss talking to Will. There, I said it.

xoxo

PS. So you and John ready for the Fling? I'm going to need some juicy reports to entertain me on dance night. No big plans for me.

From: **LottieM17@gmail.com**
Sent: Saturday, April 10, 3:30pm
To: ClaireBearR16@gmail.com
Subject: Re: Make it go away

Oh Bear, I'm so sorry that you have to go through all of this. You deserve a great guy and for a while, I think we both thought JD (or I guess, Will as JD!) was that guy. But trust me sweetie, he is out there. And I know you think that I have it all figured out with guys, but I'm beginning to realize I'm as

clueless in love as you are. As anyone is, I guess. What I DO know is that the people you should WANT to be with are the ones who see who you are—flaws and all—and stick around because of that. Don't yell—but sort of the way Will has liked you despite your paper freak-outs, JD obsessions, and horse tirades. :)

PLEASE don't be mad at me for saying this, but maybe, if you miss talking to him, you should take that as a sign. Follow your heart. That's what you always tell me. I want you to be happy.

Even though I always brush you off when you talk about what's going to happen when we go away to college and worry that we won't stay close, I know that wouldn't happen. You are my rock. My shrink. You are more than a best friend. You are my sister. So, maybe, just maybe, take what I have to say to heart.

xoxo

PS: About the Fling—I'm thinking maybe John isn't the best choice. I've been talking to Bennett a lot . . .

From: **ClaireBearR16@gmail.com**
Sent: Saturday, April 10, 6:38pm
To: LottieM17@gmail.com
Subject: You are the best!

You will never lose me! You are stuck! But while I never want to lose you as a BFF, I'm not sure I can follow my heart. Not yet. Will would need to write something worthy of a Pulitzer to get me to even listen. I'm done with boys for a while!

—Bear

PS: OMG!

ClaireRBear Longest weekend ever.
7:09am

 WiseOneWP For the first time in my life, I'm actually thankful for schoolwork. I need the distraction.
7:39am

 WiseOneWP Although schoolwork means going to school and that means signs for Fling and that means . . .
7:40am

 WiseOneWP AH! The spiral mind-games have begun again.
7:41am

 KingofSlack I LOVE spiral mind-games but not as much as I love Spinal Tap. Anybody in the mood for a good movie?
11:45am

 KingofSlack@WiseOneWP How you holding up buddy?
11:45am

 WiseOneWP@KingofSlack How do you think? Claire still isn't speaking to me. Or even glancing at me.
11:46am

 WiseOneWP@KingofSlack I mean, it was bad enough when I had to hear her talking about how much she liked JD. At least then she talked.
11:50am

WiseOneWP@KingofSlack This is way worse.
11:51am

 KingofSlack@WiseOneWP I'm sorry buddy. I know I kind of got you into this and I'm going to do what I can to help you . . . promise.
11:55am

 WiseOneWP@KingofSlack Nothing anyone can do or say is going to help me, is it?
11:59am

ClaireRBear Only two more weeks till the big dance. Then four more weeks. Then summer. Bliss.
12:10pm

 KingofSlack@ClaireRBear Can I just say something? As a friend?
12:11pm

 ClaireRBear@KingofSlack Wait, you're a friend? That's funny. In my book friends are people who don't lie to you.
12:12pm

 KingofSlack@ClaireRBear I deserve that. And I know Will and I hurt you. I owe you an apology.
12:14pm

 KingofSlack@ClaireRBear I'm sorry. Really. It got out of hand. I should have tried harder to stop it.
12:14pm

 KingofSlack@ClaireRBear Can you just hear me out? For old time's sake?
12:15pm

 ClaireRBear@KingofSlack Fine. But I want you to know I'm NEVER returning that Star Wars Episode 4 DVD that you left at my house.
12:16pm

 KingofSlack@ClaireRBear Ouch. Okay, well for now I understand. Anyway, listen, I just want u to know how upset Will is.
12:20pm

ClaireRBear@KingofSlack He's not the only one who's upset.
12:21pm

 KingofSlack@ClaireRBear Please think about this. Will likes you. A lot.
12:22pm

 KingofSlack@ClaireRBear I take that back. Will loves you. I don't think he told you that, but I know it's true.
12:23pm

 KingofSlack@ClaireRBear You are his lobster. Or swan. Or penguin. The Spock to his Kirk. My point is, you may not want to see it, but it's there.
12:25pm

 ClaireRBear@KingofSlack What? Lobster??
12:25pm

 KingofSlack@ClaireRBear You know. They mate for life, right? I'm trying to be romantic, here. Go with it.
12:26pm

 KingofSlack@ClaireRBear Why else would he listen to you go on about your dates with JD? He'd rather see you happy, even if it meant he was in pain.
12:28pm

 ClaireRBear@KingofSlack I read that's just a myth. About lobsters.
12:28pm

KingofSlack@ClaireRBear Whatever. Hear me out.
12:29pm

 KingofSlack@ClaireRBear That is why Will did what he did. Because he wants you to be happy. So, just maybe remember that.
12:29pm

 KingofSlack@ClaireRBear Hello? You still there?
12:38pm

 ClaireRBear@KingofSlack Bennett Jones, when did you get so sensitive?
12:40pm

 KingofSlack@ClaireRBear Don't tell anyone.
12:41pm

 KingofSlack@ClaireRBear So . . . are you going to give him another chance?
12:42pm

 ClaireRBear@KingofSlack I don't know. I just don't know if I can.
12:43pm

 KingofSlack@ClaireRBear I think you can. I hope you can.
12:44pm

Lots0love@KingofSlack Did you talk to Claire? She said something today about you not being such a jerk after all. Is she really coming around?
4:57pm

 Lots0love@KingofSlack I was too shocked to ask her follow-up questions.
5:00pm

 KingofSlack@Lots0love Couldn't tell you anyway. Doctor-patient confidentiality. *RT@Lots0love I was too shocked to ask her follow-up questions.*
5:01pm

 Lots0love@WiseOneWP I can't believe I'm doing this but I think you really like Claire and I think you would be good for her so . . .
5:02pm

 Lots0love@WiseOneWP She is NOT going to talk to you. Even though she wants to. You need to write something "Pulitzer worthy." That's what she says.
5:03pm

 WiseOneWP@Lots0love Thank you so much!! I have no idea what that means, but thank you. And for the record, I really do like her. A lot.
5:12pm

 Lots0love@WiseOneWP Good. Don't hurt her again. Or you will really know pain.
5:15pm

ClaireRBear Just got back from the barn. Sort of feel normal today. Maybe time does heal all wounds? Here's hoping.
5:16pm

 ClaireRBear AND my mom is out and left me with yummy leftovers. Much better mood.
5:17pm

 KingofSlack@Lots0love So . . . any more thought about going with me to fling??
5:30pm

 Lots0love@KingofSlack Whoa there turbo. You just asked me. I told you I would give you an answer by end of week. :)
5:39pm

 KingofSlack@Lots0love This is more torturous than when there was like a six month hiatus between Lost seasons. Help a man out!
5:40pm

 Lots0love@KingofSlack There is a man around? Where?
5:43pm

 KingofSlack@Lots0love Very funny. Well, I'm nothing if not stubborn. I'm going to keep bugging you until I get that answer.
5:50pm

 KingofSlack@Lots0love Bug
5:51pm

KingofSlack@Lots0love Bug

5:53pm

 KingofSlack@Lots0love Bug

5:55pm

 Lots0love@KingofSlack I'll go with you!! Now can you stop bugging me, please? I gotta go see how Claire is doing.

6:00pm

 KingofSlack I AM the king!!! Look out Fling . . . you've never seen a dancer the likes of me.

6:01pm

BIG MOUTH B

The Jig Is Up? . . . . Is anyone really surprised?

Monday, April 12, 7:37pm

I'm not going to lie to you my fine followers and first-time readers (big hallmark—just received my tenth view! Only took me 5 months—thanks Mom, for reading this nine times!). I kid. Sort of. But not about the no lies part. It is my job, nay, my DUTY, to keep you informed of all the happenings in the halls of WP, and so it is out of that obligation that I share with you now this piece news. JD is going to the Spring Fling with Jessica Mayers. GASP! I'll give you a minute to digest the news.

You good? Good. So we all knew it was going to happen. I mean, she is the reigning queen of WP and he is our undisputed king. They HAVE to go together. And after the Fling, they will have to go to prom together and then maybe date through summer and then they will break up when JD goes to USC and discovers college co-eds and Jessica will realize that these were the golden years of her reign and will slowly slip into obscurity, only able to relive the highs by looking through old yearbooks and prom pics.

And where will I be while all this is going on, you ask? Why this bitterness re: the predestined happiness of this photogenic couple? I'm not actually all that bitter. I know where I stand.

All this musing about flings has made me long to do a movie marathon of some of the greatest, angstiest high school movies made. Starting with the top one of all time—Heathers. See it. Oldie but goodie.

So while I enjoy, go out and find your own dates, and I'll see you at the Fling! Say hi, puh-lease. I'll be the guy in the corner in the ill-fitting suit. (Thanks dad for apparently NOT passing along your broad shoulders and narrow waist genes. The spider body look is OH-SO attractive on me!)

Wait, did I say ill-fitting suit? I meant I'll be the guy in the corner, in the ill-fitting suit, with the smoking hot DATE!

Tuesday, April 13, 2010

THE MAGIC 8 BALL IN MY HEAD . . .

Due to some positive feedback on my short-answer "Magic 8 Ball" approach to my own questions, I'm going to tackle some of yours in the same manner. Well, not entirely. This will be more of a team effort—a mind meld, if you will, between girl and mysterious spherical object. (What *is* that stuff the answers float in?) This time around I'm going to only rely *partly* on the Magic 8 Ball of Stupidity. He'll answer (yes, it is a he—explains the short, unemotional responses) and then I'll add some of my own thoughts to the mix of cluelessness. Enjoy.

> **Dear Clueless,**
> **If everyone else is going to a dance and I don't have a date, should I stay home or go stag?**
> **—Cinderella Without a Prince**

The answer is: Without a doubt.

Oh Magic 8 Ball, what kind of answer is that? The human answer is: Stag! Any school dance I've gone to I've gone with my best guy friend so I'm not much help—again. But I say go! Even if you don't have a date, who dances with their date, anyway? Although, if you and some other friends can make alternate plans, that is an option too. So is my current plan: watching marathons of VH1 reality shows. But that can get depressing. Trust me.

Dear Clueless,
My parents hate my boyfriend. They think he's stupid and that he's going to break my heart. Should I break up with him? Or should I go with my gut and stay with him?
                                        —Heartache

The answer is: Reply hazy, try again.

Apparently Mr. Magic 8 is not feeling the magic— or the love—today. To add my thoughts here—I think the hazy part of his answer is because separating gut from heart is a difficult thing to do. But I'm learning that going with your gut is usually wise. I said usually.

Dear Clueless,
I found out that my boyfriend was seeing another girl while we were going out. I broke up with him, but now he is begging me to come back. I feel like he has violated my trust. Do I take him back?

The answer is: My reply is no.

For once I can't argue with the 8 Ball. What would be the point of trying to trust your boyfriend again? I worry you'd be setting yourself up for more hurt.

ClaireRBear Is going to get her head back on track and her heart in line. No more silly infatuation
Tuesday, April 13, 12:05pm

 ClaireRBear Can't believe her best friend has fallen for the most unexpected guy in the world!
12:05pm

 Lots0love@ClaireRBear Keep it down girl!! I don't want Benn to know I like him too much. Need to keep him guessing.
12:09pm

 ClaireRBear@Lots0love LOL! I don't think he needs to guess much. And hey, if u found actual real guy who makes u all aflutter . . . why hide it?
12:12pm

 Lots0love@ClaireRBear I could say the same thing about you, my dear.
12:13pm

 ClaireRBear@Lots0love Not the same. Not really. I mean, I will admit there was a small part of me that might once have felt flutters for Will. Once.
12:15pm

 Lots0love@ClaireRBear I wish there was something I could do to make you feel magically better.
12:17pm

 Lots0love@ClaireRBear I'll miss you at the dance. This will be first year we both don't go
12:20pm

Lots0love@ClaireRBear Not that it matters, but I think JD was actually pretty bummed. Obviously you were the best thing that ever happened to him.
12:21pm

 ClaireRBear@Lots0love Sure I was. I would have been as big a liar as Will if I'd gone. You have to send me pics and texts from fling please.
12:22pm

 Lots0love@ClaireRBear You could come with us!
12:23pm

 ClaireRBear@Lots0love I'm not sure I'm up for playing 3rd wheel. But thanks for invite. I'm sure there is a marathon on USA to watch.
12:25pm

 ClaireRBear@Lots0love Why am I so confused? And why does that make me feel funny?
12:26pm

 Lots0love@ClaireRBear I dunno kiddo. But remember, love doesn't always make sense . . . or happen the way you expect. *RT@ClaireRBear Why am I so confused?*
12:28pm

 WiseOneWP@ClaireRBear I wrote something for you. Hope you have an answer for me.
12:30pm

Tuesday, April 13, 2010

A GREAT BIG MESS . . .

Just one letter to respond to today. I hope you'll agree with me that it deserves a column of its own. I just wish I knew how to answer.

> **Dear Get Clueless,**
> I need your help. I've screwed up. In a big big way. There is a girl that I love and, well, I made a great big mess of things.
> Here's my story. I liked a girl who liked someone else. So I pretended to be that person. It wasn't wise, or particularly kind, but more than I wanted her to love me back, I wanted this girl to be happy. Unfortunately, in trying to be a hero to a girl who meant the world to me, I proved myself to be a greater jerk than I ever imagined I could.
> I tried to fix it. I tried to tell the girl I love that I miss the warmth of her smile. I tried to tell her she made me want to be funny so I could hear her laugh. And it's true. I want her

to have nothing but staircase moments and doors opened for her. I want her to realize that she is the least clueless girl I know. That she is bright and beautiful. Right now, I would do anything just to hear her say my name, and I would give anything if she would look at me again and smile. But I don't know if that's possible.

Please tell me, Claire. What can I do?

How can I fix this when saying I love you is not enough?

—Will Parker

Dear Will Parker,

Thanks for writing me. I checked the Magic 8 Ball. It says Cannot predict now. Perhaps if you check back in person, the answer will be different.

Lots0love@ClaireRBear So . . . nice question, huh?

1:00pm

 ClaireRBear@Lots0love Hard to miss. I can't believe he did that!

1:05pm

 Lots0love@ClaireRBear So are you going to forgive him? Said you couldn't predict. But he loves you, Claire. He basically told the whole school!

1:09pm

 ClaireRBear@Lots0love Give me a minute to think, would ya? It's a lot for a girl to take in.

1:15pm

 ClaireRBear@Lots0love Okay, wrote up list of pros and cons. Pros: Friend, funny, cute, gangly walk, raises one eyebrow when he smiles, likes me for me.

1:20pm

 ClaireRBear@Lots0love Cons: He lied to me.

1:21pm

 Lots0love@ClaireRBear Oh Claire. What are you waiting for? You like him too.

1:22pm

 ClaireRBear@Lots0love I do, don't I? This is so weird. It's Will. And I mean, can I really ever get past the lying thing?

1:23pm

Lots0love@ClaireRBear I'm not sure, but I think you have to try. Let yourself fall, Claire. He'll catch ya.

1:24pm

ClaireRBear@Lots0love I'm going to think about this. I'll call you when I get home . . .
1:25pm

 KingofSlack@Lots0love Hey Lottie . . . I sent you something. Check your email.
3:01pm

 Lots0love@KingofSlack If you sent me another link to guys holding iPhones and doing weird things, I am officially un-following you.
3:02pm

 KingofSlack@Lots0love Just check for crying out loud you difficult minx!
3:05pm

 Lots0love@KingofSlack Is that how you talk to all your dates?
3:06pm

 KingofSlack@Lots0love No, only the really special ones who will let me dance like a dork at spring fling.
3:10pm

 KingofSlack@Lots0love Wait! You totally just called yourself my date! Without any bugging required. That word has a nice official ring to it, I gotta say.
3:14pm

 Lots0love@KingofSlack Yeah, the world sure is full of surprises.
3:18pm

Lots0love@KingofSlack Hey B . . . ?
3:20pm

 KingofSlack@Lots0love Yes . . .
3:21pm

 Lots0love@KingofSlack I like you.
3:22pm

 KingofSlack@Lots0love I like you, too. Lots.
3:23pm

Lots0love Fling is officially set. April 23. 6:00 dinner. 7:30 dance. Woot woot! **#dancethenightaway**
6:04pm

 Lots0love I would like to point out that only our school would have a big dance on a Friday night right before placement exams
6:05pm

 ClaireRBear@Lots0love Never fear, there is always prom my dear. You can get your wild and crazy dance on then
6:10pm

 Lots0love@ClaireRBear Maybe by that time, you'll be there with your own date and we can **#dancethenightaway**
6:12pm

 ClaireRBear@Lots0love I wouldn't count on it. Will hasn't said anything to me since the article.
6:14pm

 Lots0love@ClaireRBear Maybe he is waiting for you to say something. Think he kind of put himself out there already
6:17pm

 ClaireRBear@Lots0love What if he changed his mind? Or what if this is all one big mistake? Or what if I can never really forgive him?
6:20pm

Lots0love@ClaireRBear Time will tell my friend. But only way to know is if you try . . .
6:21pm

 ClaireRBear@Lots0love True enough. You really are a love guru.
6:23pm

 WiseOneWP@ClaireRBear Hey. You got a minute to talk? I was going to be in the neighborhood . . .
6:30pm

 ClaireRBear@Lots0love Speak of the devil!! Will just tweeted. He wants to come over . . .
6:32pm

 Lots0love@ClaireRBear Go! Talk to him! Then call me!
6:35pm

 ClaireRBear@Lots0love Okay Bossyface! Tweeting him now.
6:37pm

ClaireRBear@WiseOneWP Hey, I'm here. Wanna come over?

6:38pm

 WiseOneWP@ClaireRBear I can't think of anything I'd like more.

6:39pm

 ClaireRBear@WiseOneWP Before you run for the door, I do have one question.

6:41pm

 WiseOneWP@ClaireRBear Shoot.

6:41pm

 ClaireRBear@WiseOneWP That night, at Benn's, when I was crying about my father, I wanted you to hug me. You, not JD. Why didn't you?

6:43pm

 WiseOneWP@ClaireRBear I wanted to. I should have. I've never seen you look more beautiful.

6:45pm

 ClaireRBear@WiseOneWP What? My face was all blotchy. I was completely gross.

6:46pm

 WiseOneWP@ClaireRBear You. Were. Beautiful. You are ALWAYS beautiful.

6:46pm

 ClaireRBear@WiseOneWP Hey, Will?

6:50pm

WiseOneWP@ClaireRBear Yes?
6:51pm

 ClaireRBear@WiseOneWP Come on over. But just be yourself, okay?
6:52pm

 **WiseOneWP@ClaireRBear** From here on out. Promise.
6:53pm

From: **ClaireBearR16@gmail.com**
Sent: Wednesday, April 14, 11:57pm
To: LottieM17@gmail.com
Subject: See you at the fling

Dearest, most wonderful, and lovely Lottie,
You'll be happy to know that after an appropriate amount of begging and pleading, I have forgiven Will.

He came over and told me the whole story. While I still don't fully understand what on earth was he thinking (nor do I think I ever will), I'm coming around to the idea that he sort of did it out of misplaced loyalty.

Anyway, I wanted you to be the first to know—I'm going to the Fling with Will. I have no idea what will happen between him and me. I don't know if we will make it to graduation, much less to next year. And I've never been more excited or scared, ever. Period. But I'm following my heart. So, wanna double date?

xoxo
Bear

BIG MOUTH B

Happily Ever After . . . (seriously, this is it!)

Saturday, April 24, 11:31am

The Fling has flung, the song is done, and for once, Big Mouth has nothing snarky to say. Why, you ask? Because the mouth himself is recovering from a sprained ankle—apparently doing the shopping cart is more dangerous than one would think—and I, Claire Collins, have taken over for one entry. I know a little something about pretending, after all.

So while Bennett recovers, I'm going to give you a little story to send you off to sleep. A love story if you will . . . and this one has a happy ending:

I knew he was waiting downstairs. I could hear him talking to my mother. The sound of his voice made me smile.

My best friend had come over earlier to help me get dolled up, though she spent most of the time typing furiously on her phone—most likely to her date. Who would have believed the lax queen would settle down with the resident sci-fi dork of WP? It fits, though. And she deserves to be happy. But now I was alone in my room, my heart thudding and my hands all clammy.

I heard my mother call me from downstairs. I took a deep breath and walked out of my room. This was it—I was about to go on a date with the guy who had been my buddy for years, lied to me, broken my heart, and then stolen it right back. I stood at the top of the stairs.

He was waiting at the bottom, nervously playing with the corsage in his hand. My mother, bless her heart (for real!), had left us alone. The top step squeaked beneath my weight and he looked up. He grinned and I felt my heart leap in response. Step by step I made my way down, managing not to stumble even once. When I was at the bottom, you know what he did? He held out his arm and said, "May I have this staircase moment?"

I leaned toward him, and before I could rethink the impulse, I kissed him. I felt his surprise, and then he kissed me back. It was a first kiss and an apology kiss and a forgiveness kiss, all rolled into one. And it was perfect.

He pulled back and smiled, his green eyes mirroring my own surprise and happiness. I laughed, too afraid to talk just yet. I figured we had plenty of time for that. At the Fling. The summer. Maybe all of senior year. For now, I just wanted to get back to what we had been doing. Why? Because, I was getting my first real kiss—and the guy? He was definitely my very own tweet heart.

Acknowledgments

Bringing a novel in tweets to life turned out to be a lot harder than I imagined. Partly because it happened pretty much overnight.

Thank you, first, to my amazing agent, Faye Bender, who was willing to go with the flow when I dumped *Tweet Heart* unceremoniously into her inbox and said "help." Her encouragement kept me going through the tough times and made me believe in my characters. Many thanks to my fantastic and patient editor, Abby Ranger, who stuck by me through A LOT of revisions and not very much time to do them in. Her insight, guidance, and witty one-liners helped shape this book into something with an actual beginning, middle, and end.

Of course the book would never have happened without Stephanie Lurie, David Epstein, my amazing bosses Rich Thomas and Wendy Lefkon, Beth Clark for her twitteriffic design, Sara Liebling for keeping the book on track, Nisha Panchal for giving me all the bells and whistles, Monica Mayper for tweaking tweet, and the rest of the team at Hyperion, who took a risk on an editor who wanted to write.

Then there were those poor unfortunate souls who served as early readers and sounding boards. Thanks to Colin Hosten, who was my own help desk for all things Twitter, and the inspiration behind much of the book. And to Marianne Schaberg, who suffered through high school with me, taught me the fine art of sarcasm, and still dared to read my book, give me great feedback, and help me laugh when I wanted to flip out. Of course, I couldn't have done any of this without my author friends Helen Perelman, Kathryn Williams, and James Ponti, who all helped me be a stronger writer by forcing me to push myself and my work to their level. I can only hope I came close. And to my junior year English teacher, Anne Shaunessy, who taught me not only to love the written word, but also the fine art of rewriting—something that came in plenty handy while working on *Tweet Heart*.

I also owe thanks to Amy Alessi, Dana Bornstein, and Christopher Viaggio, who let me plaster their pictures all through the book—the real life versions of Claire, Lottie, and Will.

Finally, for their love and support during this whole experience; my parents, Lynn and Seth Rudnick, who gave up their dining room table for much of the summer to let me write for hours on end; my brother, Ben, for having the high school experience I never had and giving me lots of good material for the kids of Watkins; and most special thanks to my own Jack Dyson, whose big puppy dog eyes are as cute as JD's.